AM I ALONE

IN THE WORLD?

GREGORY J. LAUGHERY

Destinée

Am I Alone in the World?

© 2022 Gregory J. Laughery

Published by Destinée Media www.destineemedia.com

Written by Gregory J. Laughery

ISBN: 978-1-938367-69-4

I've been writing this story for about six years and it's finally finished. Many thanks to those who read through early drafts and offered comments. I'm especially grateful for my wife Elizabeth (Lisby). She spent hours on this project. Her insightful contributions and remarkable editing skills made this a much better book. Any remaining errors are mine.

For the full experience reading this novel, listen to the fabulous music of Nils Frahm, Max Richter, and Ólafur Arnalds.

There's an ineffable dimension to this story, but I must tell you something. So, here it goes.

Planet Earth was suffering under the weight of climate change, widespread pollution, and devastating exploitation. Due to the rising temperatures the polar ice melted and the oceans expanded becoming frighteningly unpredictable for navigation, while at the same time flooding many areas. Oil spills increased, toxic waste multiplied, and nuclear plant meltdowns proliferated. Deforestation continued, fresh water supplies diminished, massive fires raged, and the remaining land was pillaged for its resources and left barren. Biodiversity and the ecosystem were battered beyond recognition by a suite of pesticides, refuse, and genetic manipulation. Famine and pandemics followed and plagued the entire Earth. Everything was disintegrating and rapidly on its way to total collapse. Death stars, asteroids, meteorites, comets, black holes and dark matter were powerful forces and a constant menace. Alongside this, hyper-technology and artificial intelligence ran rampant. Clones, robots, borgs, and drones boomed. They were all over the place; controlling, spying, and invading private human spaces. The threat to human and animal existence grew more rapidly than anyone had imagined. Many species had disappeared and thousands of others were on the brink of destruction. Panic and fear were prominent in people's lives and worked its way into the global centers of politics and the world economy. The mantra of dread was everywhere and repeated over and over again by the fear peddling media. Had billions of years of evolution now brought us to this? While several mass extinctions had already taken place, the last one approximately sixty-six million years ago with roughly seventy-five per cent of plants and animals wiped out, a similar scenario for the world as humans knew it, now seemed inevitable.

The extinction of all life forms was at hand. Yet, history had repeatedly shown us that the Earth and more recently humanity had a striking capacity to survive, even in tragic and catastrophic circumstances. In the face of impending disaster, would both somehow manage to do so again?

Or was it too late?

Suddenly, there are massive explosions and violent earthquakes. The ground shakes and breaks loose from under my feet. I have only a split second to think, and I attempt to scan what is happening, but it's impossible in this sliver of time to assess my situation. I don't have a clue. I'm stunned and losing my balance, I fall, or lapse into another state of consciousness or is it unconsciousness? Something like that.

Then, it seems as if I go into shock, and my whole world is now vastly different than it ever appeared to be before. I gradually regain my composure, though somewhat staggered, but nothing is broken or bleeding. I stumble around and attempt to check things out. Complete chaos appears to have been unleashed. I wander from one place to another, still dazed and confused, and after some time, how much I'll never know, I notice, as far as I can tell, that I am alone, I think. I just don't see anyone else around. This is strange, even eerie, to say the least. Trust me, the imaginative sensation of being alone in the world is an anxious and frightening experience. Where is everybody? Why am I still here when nobody else seems to be?

When some more time has passed, how much I can't tell, I become anxious about how to survive my present predicament. But, what predicament? Survival, survival, and survival is all that goes through my mind. Breathing is difficult and strength is low. By all appearances, I'm here by myself. I want to know what the hell transpired and left me in these circumstances. Not sure I'll ever find out, but who knows what will emerge? Other questions arise: where can I find food and shelter?

What should I do now? Why am I here? I glance around me. There are collapsed buildings, empty streets, and plenty of ground and space craft pieces scattered about. Trees are uprooted, lamp posts down on the ground, and communication infrastructures entirely dysfunctional. A smoky blackish gray residue floats in the air. I scramble up a huge pile of debris to get some perspective. As far as I can see, the place is in total ruins.

Maybe the entire world is like this.

Who knows?

This is a perplexing, even haunting thought. Nothing seems to be like it once was. It is as if everything is in a perpetual state of emergency, yet no one is around except me to alert to the present force of danger. Danger? The dusty vapor of destruction is plain enough to see, but what does all this mean?

At first I ramble around aimlessly, then I intentionally begin to search for food and drink. I'm famished and thirsty. I desperately look around, but find nothing to fill my empty stomach or quench my thirst. I eventually stumble onto what must have previously been a small shop. I crawl in under the broken beams and through masses of clutter and after uncovering some rubble and scrounging around I'm able to find a few pieces of rice like brown crackers, and water gushing from a broken tap. I think to myself: Ok, good for now and then eat and drink. After this, back outside I go.

I wonder about how I can find the explanation for my current state of affairs and how I'm going to survive it. Bewildering. Panicky, I forge on through the gloomy vacant streets now flooded in darkness. There are no lights shining anywhere within my vicinity; stone cold dark. Someone must be around. Power outage? Definitely, but surely more than that! A strong odor of something rotting pervades my senses.

Humans? Animals? Not sure. I have no idea.

My hands are tightly jammed in the pockets of my black pants and my shoulders hunched up against the glacial cold. It's freezing. Walking more quickly now from street to street, or what is left of them, nothing changes. I keep expecting a light, some warmth, and to escape the stench. Same darkness, same cold, same smell. What's happening here? It looks like some post-apocalyptic scenario, but where am I?

Recognizing that, at this moment, I'm immersed in that which I didn't choose or determine, I become even more unsettled and rather distressed. For some reason, memories of doing it on my own and being independent ripple through me.

Who am I now? Identity? Identity? Why am I alone?

I used to somehow be able to pretend I was in charge. I assumed I was a capital 'I.' The master of my life. Certain, authoritative, and powerful. No longer. In actuality, I now think, I'm so fragile and vulnerable, affected by all that's in and around me. I'm dust, lasting no longer than grass and flowers in the field. I will all too soon disappear. But then, I realize that I'm still here, experiencing fear, feeling cold, and smelling death, and pangs of loneliness and insecurity overwhelm me. I wander around desperately searching for signs of life, which appear to have vanished, leaving me with utter absence.

Terrified, I press on.

I trudge through loads of rubble that are strewn all over. This literal scene metaphorically resembles some of the relational contexts of my own life. What a mess. I used to think that some people were hell. I detested the superficial drabble about the weather or the hum drum state of work. I thought then, get a life.

But now after being alone for some time, how long I'm not sure, even the trite comments of another person would be welcome. I long for human contact. A voice. A touch. A face. I'm desperate. Then, in my stupor, I realize I hear someone. At first, there are only muffled words. Hope and excitement flow through me. My heart feels like it will explode. Even though it is freezing, I strip off my tattered blue coat and begin to uncover some of the wreckage with my hands. Pieces of concrete and broken glass are piled up. I carefully remove them one by one. I then quickly realize that the voice I hear is not a breathing fleshly being as I am, but a newfangled no-battery cell phone, repeating over and over: "the person you have called is not available - try calling again later."

Terrified, I press on.

Daylight is gradually emerging. Gray billowing smoke on the horizon tinged with reds, oranges, and blues makes me wonder what kind of day, if you could call it that, this is going to be. Progressively, I try to relax, which is welcoming for the nerves, body, and mind. I then put on my blue coat again and stick my hands back in my pockets to attempt to get warm. I turn right and head up the street, or at least what I think was once a street.

Hard to tell!

So much around me looks the same, and I begin to see that it is going to be difficult to escape the sense of being caught in a sort of labyrinth with no way out. At that moment, discussions I once had about language being a never ending series of signs without referent or meaning flow into my mind. I think, well, this is what that's really like, except in a visual, spatial manner. I can't even distinguish one street from another. Pitiful. But why does it matter? I don't know. In one way nothing at all matters, in another way everything does.

Now that it is a bit lighter, I think there must be a way to find out where I am and why things are such a mess. I need news. I want information. Solitude and emptiness don't explain my condition and what I see around me. Cautiously, I head further up the street, or what is left of it. My pursuit for signs of life is unsuccessful, which brings me back to wondering what the hell is going on. Baffled. Confused. I strive to find an explanation for all this.

The constant banter inside me seems to flow in five or six directions at once. Keep going, moving, and searching. Quit, give up, and stay put. Survival is all that counts. But, for what? Why? Tension is mounting within me, and I'm not sure how to cope with this raw emotion. I scream and holler to unwind a bit. And listen to the sound of my voice. That works for now.

Deciding to carry on, I go through a hole in the side of what's left of a drab cement building. This structure is grayish brown and must have been an uncreative block or square style place used for housing. Looks like a laser blast has blown it apart, but who knows? Coming out the other side, I discover a kaleidoscope of colors; mesmerizingly beautiful, but they dissolve in a matter of seconds without a trace.

A mirage?

My wish at that moment is that I had more detailed insight into neuroscience. I know the human brain is powerful and has plasticity, but could it possibly connect with dimensions beyond the visual? Maybe what I'm experiencing is a brain thing. While this may be the case, the destitution that surrounds me seems very real. No, this is not just me I think, there's something there outside of me. But I still ask myself: I can't be constructing all this in my mind, can I?

As I continue to pursue a reason for this emptiness of the world, I unexpectedly come across an almost fully standing wall. It is covered in graffiti – or art work, as some have called it. Were these messages of hope, despair, or protest that shed light on what might have been about to happen? A sort of prophetic picture of what had now taken place? Humanity and the environment were in danger of extinction, and artists were often on the cutting edge of insight, and even revelation. Wow! Can I decipher anything pertinent here?

Then something mind blowing happens. I hear what seems like a blast of trumpets playing one sustained note, and in the background a choir of voices linger, rising and falling. This is overwhelming and breathtaking. Kind of like the force of rushing wind or water – an eerie feeling of being taken away, a long ways away.

Crushingly sublime!

Never heard anything like this, and as it gradually and unfortunately fades, I'm left enthralled in front of the wall of graffiti. What in the world?

When the exhilaration of such a magnificent acoustic encounter subsides, I start paying more detailed attention to the colorfully sublime wall art. While the wall is a sort of neutral beige, the vibrant colors of the letters and designs stream out like adrenaline-charged rainbows; reds, yellows, blues, and greens. There is an aesthetic dimension to the graffiti that is somehow both shocking and soothing.

Tensional intrigue captures my feelings. Wow! Much of what I see and read seems to express graphic outrage about the dehumanizing forces that were taking over planet Earth. Corruption, climate change, and poverty, seemed to be their most prominent concerns, though there were others, such as nuclear war, AI technology, and surveillance. Techno-sapiens, robots, and borgs, as it was graffitied, controlled vast amounts of territory. Human life faced multiple threats, including the power and folly of these pseudo-beings. The irony, in my view, was that humans had become enslaved to their own techno creations, and in doing so lost much of their humanity. And ethics and accountability were down the toilet. According to these striking and colorful signs on the wall, the world was in grave danger, and in that sense they were truly prophetic, but regrettably they don't take me much further towards understanding what happened next and why I appear to be alone.

The illuminating experience of the past moments or hours, who knows how long it was, makes me want to somehow climb into the wall, and engage with these artists.

Strange?

Well, yes, yes. I desperately desire to become part of its revealing story; life lived as narrative art, yet I have to forge ahead to the future, unknown as it might be. Moving away from the wall and the imaginative space that had opened up, leaves me feeling frustrated and sad. I nevertheless remain determined to continue my search. While I had once heard it said somewhere that the world was a theater of possibilities, nothing of the kind now seems to be the case for me.

Turning what looks like a corner, I wander along and pass through a broken archway that leads me into a marvelous courtyard with brick paved streets. The buildings inside are torn apart and many of them have entirely buckled. Rotted wood and what looks like the remains of flower boxes are scattered around. This, at one time, must have been a place of idyllic serenity and remarkable beauty. A haven, perhaps, but now it is a lost refuge. I sit and reflect. What was it that ripped the guts out of everything I could see? Such powers of destruction appear to have been a mighty force, though I still can't tell who they were or where they came from.

Terrified, I press on.

Then I head up a convoluted street that ripples like a mini roller coaster. While I'm getting somewhat used to the awful smell and the terrible cold, they remain vexing and make me even more uncomfortable in my skin. I feel like I'm sick and going to barf, but alas it's more a sensation than an actual event. I hope you know what I mean. Sometimes you can have this strange sense that something has come over you, and it sinks into your bones, and stagnates, and lingers. It shrouds you like a massive weight that doesn't let up. Ugh. You imagine vomiting would be a relief, but it doesn't happen. Flesh and blood may not be the best form of existence, I reflect, but it's the best I have to survive my surroundings, though I do wonder about the value of sustaining a life alone in the world.

So, where shall I go now? Which direction from here?

I then break through the ruins and the collapsed thick doors of a cathedral thinking I might perhaps find a secret message left behind here for whoever may have survived the devastation. I search around looking for codes or clues, maybe a record of an apocalyptic vision. I turn over parts of wooden pews that are not buried, explore what appears to be the remains of the altar, but I gradually realize that it is highly unlikely I will find anything. There are mounds of gorgeous stones and beautiful tiles piled up all over and who knows how deep the debris actually is. As I move further into this monument, I notice off to the side there is a grand Steinway piano. Scrambling over for a closer look I'm astonished to find that this magnificent instrument has pretty much been preserved from the wreckage since it sat under an arch, a more solid piece of the cathedral structure. Amazingly, the piano is playable and even in tune.

Mind blowing!

I start to play. What comes out is a beautiful haunting sound expressing an intense harmonic sphere that reflects my present emotions of being torn between life and death. Playing the music brings forth a sort of catharsis that evokes a state of euphoria, which carries me into a deep vortex of visual intrigue. I see a tunnel like structure arrayed with torches that light the way to the end. It leads to a large room that looks like it is made of multi-colored glass, some frosted, some clear. There in the midst of the walled edifice are sort of creature like beings – whether they have ontology or not I'll probably never know – who are performing some type of rite to a central figure that appears to be machine like, rather than flesh and blood. Creepy feelings crawl through my skin and then the scene is gone, and I'm back at the piano in the cathedral.

Phew! – What was that? A vision - symbol; some sort of message?

A mere brain phenomenon?

Maybe these experiences are going to help in my search to find out what is going on. Maybe not.

I continue to play the piano until it brings me to a place where I feel a surge of new energy. I think I should now move on and explore further, though I would like continue playing on and on and on. Crawling out of the collapsed cathedral is an arduous and complex feat, but I eventually find my way back to the mini roller coaster like street. Leaving the cathedral leaves me feeling naked inside. My insecurity is becoming more tangible, yet I'm compelled to pursue a better understanding of the life I now experience. Perhaps, I should give up on this seemingly foolish quest, but I don't yet feel quite ready to do that. Soon, maybe, but not now.

I look up and down the mini roller coaster street and decide to head up. It is still freezing and the smell is still awful. When will it change? Is something more pleasant realistic to hope for or am I stuck in a rhythm of desolate monotony that goes on and on and on? I think to myself this is what death must be – monotony, though without being aware of it. You'd never be able to tell. No contact, no connection, no possibility. Kind of like a record that is stuck in the same place and repeats itself over and over and over. As for me, I somehow need to conjure up a good dose of romantic optimism, but in my circumstances that is hard to come by, and perhaps not even a very welcome alternative. 'I just don't know' is becoming easier and easier to say than it ever has been before. Phew!

As I amble up a previously populated, but now empty roller coastered rippled street, suddenly four streaming square shapes appear, each of a different color; blue, red, yellow, and white. Are these a reflection of something? Is there a reason for these particular colors and in this four-sided form? Random? I guess so. Not sure.

But whatever the source of this visionary experience, which is indeed mysterious, for me it's like a neuro event. These colorful cubes somehow give me a jolt of vitality. My strength and energy increase some, and I'm able to pick up my journey on what appears to me to be the forsaken side of the planet Earth. The cubes fade away, just as fast as they appeared.

Moving further along the cracked road, which I navigate for the moment without too much difficulty, I find that as much as the material world is a phenomenon I have to pay attention to, I'm equally, or even more so at times, living within my imagination.

This is such an intense and present focus it almost dominates my state of being. It's remarkable how inner vision and outer seeing can be so distinct, yet so related. This reminds me of long interesting discussions that I used to have with family and friends about the 'real' world. I remember back then having considered the reflections of many past thinkers, including two that got things going on this question: Plato and Aristotle.

What is real?

Plato, one of the key figures in western thought, delves into the important question of image and reality. He leads to us believe that reason is primary for discovering the real, while image dilutes it. To imagine or create images, according to Plato, is a further impoverishment of a material world that is already a copy of a set of transcendent ideal forms. Reason directs us into what is noble and enlightening, versus image and imagination, which leave us impoverished and in darkness. The role of the imagination, for Plato, is thus negative and leads us away from the real. And then there was Aristotle, a student of Plato and an important thinker in his own right.

What is real?

For Aristotle, images are not external expressions or copies, but internal mental representations that are connected to the senses and the mind. Far from images being false or a negation of the real, Aristotle suggests that it is not an other worldly set of ideal forms that gives us meaning, but rather it is the things in this world that are real.

I wonder just how much of a role imagination plays in human observation and understanding of what is real, and is there anything really real, independent of human imagination? The perennial struggle to understand imagination and reality was right at the heart of the work of many poets, scientists, philosophers, and theologians throughout the centuries. Ancient thinkers and bards disputed the capacity of imagination in creating or connecting to the world, while contemporary scientists and artists ponder its role in making or discovering meaning. Over the course of thousands of years, the efforts to figure out whether imagination was destructive or useful remained unresolved. So, what is real? And how might imagination be connected to this question? As much as all this fascinates me, and to some extent I can't help but reflecting on it, I have to try to channel my energy and focus into finding out what I'm experiencing and why. I seem to keep gravitating to the past and memories, somewhat elusive though they be, as the present and the future don't appear to offer a direction and any legitimate purpose.

Or, do they?

I guess things are perhaps more complex than I can fathom at any given moment. But for now what beckons me is survival and an explanation for my state and that of the planet. I can't help but add this: I wish I had some closure.

The demand for closure it seems is always interfered with by the tantalizing enigma of ending, which leaves it all open to deeper reflection. Some have said this is a universe of signifiers with no signified. Everything, it is argued, points back to itself, making exposing the secret of signifying less a promise and more a never ending process. Literature, or at least some of it, has the audacious capacity to ask questions about the world, but frequently gives few answers. I'd wager that's where I now am, in a story, a sort of or something like a de-plotted drama without denouement.

Then out of nowhere there is a ghastly scream so shrill it is like a sharp two-edged sword piercing bone and marrow. I try to cover my ears with my hands, but it is as if the sound is in my heart, more of a feeling than a blast of exterior noise. I desperately want it to stop. It immediately spikes gruesome images of suffering and horror, as well as screams of embodied psychological torture and the shock of bloody bodies scattered all over.

Stop! Please stop!

And beyond my expectations, it does. The sensation of being immersed in an awful Greek tragedy or some other calamity slowly diminishes, and I gradually return to a state of cautious terror.

Following these thoughts and experiences, I gather myself together some, and continue up the rippled street. Immediately something catches my eye. I'm drawn into a picturesque scene via a lovely broken window pane. I amble over to the splintered glass opening to have a closer look, and a blue angel like figure appears amidst the devastating wreckage. The color of this ghostly disembodied form is absolutely breathtaking. I'm not sure how to describe it. Never quite experienced such a rich, textured, and deep blue. Absolutely stunning. This beguiling character looks as if it is summoning me to enter into another "possible world" through the framed shards of glass, but I'm reluctant. Speak, I request, speak, say something. No response. Then, mesmerized, I decide to slowly move in closer, but all at once the blue angel disappears from view – too late for me to follow. Could I have joined the blue character and shared its state of being, material as I am, with a body and flesh? Or experience another "possible world?" I'd wager, at this stage, it would have been better than this one, but I don't know and really can't be sure. Sure? How can I be sure of anything in this complex mess?

At any rate, I feel like I missed my chance. I move on with a sense of regret. Perhaps, I had not been brave enough to forge through the broken window and escape into another world.

After drifting around for some time, who knows how long, I sit with my thoughts and wonder. What's it all about? I had raised this question many times before in my life, but in the midst of my present plight, it hit me more acutely. Over the years I had explored and re-explored it from a philosophical, theological, ethical, and scientific angle, debating the issues at great length. I had arrived at provisional understandings, and tentatively built on those. I loved delving into the problems of interpretation, God(s), morals, and nature. The major drawback this time, is that I have no one to discuss or engage with. Fascinating thoughts recycle within me and I find myself in a constant back and forth debating with myself. What is knowledge? Justified true belief? What is transparent or enigmatic? And God? And if God, what God? The scientific informer, points us to the vastness of the universe or is it multiverse, as well as to the miniscule details of atoms and cells, and where was God in all this?

And reality? What in the world could that be and how would I know? And what about objectivity and subjectivity? I just do not have enough information. I desperately long for shafts of light to pierce through the darkness of not knowing. But nothing is illuminating my quest. Yet, I'm starting to get used to this, and to accept that there are far more questions than answers.

I decide to get up and move on. This unfamiliar nomadic state of being is beginning to wear me down, yet I have to keep going. Survival beckons. Fate, chance, or who knows what has brought me to this particular point. And what comes next is perplexing. I had heard it said somewhere that though you may not know where the journey is heading, the important thing is to embrace it. Well, for me, this seems more foolhardy now than it ever did, as it's the destination, not the journey that counts. Where am I going though, remains a vexing question.

Turning out to the left for a while, who knows how long, I take several detours around piles of junk, gaping cracks, and huge holes in what used to be streets. The gushing water from some of the broken pipes has slowed down and this makes it a little easier to navigate, though the terrain is still treacherous. This extremely uneven landscape requires lots of work for little gain. On my way, I notice various pieces of warped edifices that randomly form interesting mosaics; fledgling beauty, I suppose, in the midst of drab debris.

Suddenly, out of the corner of my eye I catch a flicker of someone or something. I quickly turn my head and see a rather small complex colorful pattern. Turns out, it is an exquisite lure dancing in the breeze. I stand, and stand, and stand, mesmerized by this tantalizing vision. It is as if this experience takes me into a safe space so far away, yet so close, that I don't want to leave. After I almost fall over from my engagement with this transcendent thing, or whatever it might be, I come back to my very physical environment and decide it's best to depart. I wonder if what just happened to me is something like an imagination forged out of the body experience or a neuro event, perhaps similar to how some pseudo-humans, who have an ultra-fine implant in their brains connected to AI view the world. I'd wager it was a confluence of the two and maybe a whole lot more.

Who knows?

Leaving this remarkable scene behind, I plod on. It is still freezing and the awful smell continues to pervade my senses, though my body and brain are gradually adapting. I find the sensation of being alone in the world to be overwhelming, yet the drive for survival and the search for a glimmer of understanding my situation, at least at this moment, are stronger.

To my right, I now notice another collapsed structure, slightly more identifiable than many of the others. I'd guess this had been some kind of high tech lab. Strewn about are steel and plastic parts, bolts and screws. Looks like pieces of computers, machines, drones, and robots are piled up in the hundreds. I will never know for sure if pseudo-sapiens were being made at this location or by whom, but it seems highly probable judging by the vast amount and nature of material scattered around.

To what effect remains an open question. Was this sort of development simply the next step in the evolutionary process of the planet, or was it the beginning of the end?

Or neither?

A weird thought runs through my mind. Have humans made too much of themselves? It seems to me that we have the tendency to think of our race as all important, and the center of the universe. Everything, humans assume, revolves around them. But can we help it? With brains like ours perhaps it is inevitable that we view ourselves as the pinnacle of a long evolutionary history. Yet, are there surprises still to come? Neuroscience, genetics, and technology are already game changers. Never before has science been able to tell the story of the world to this extent, though somehow science alone fails to offer a sufficient means for understanding and explaining a fuller picture of life. But has science been, maybe even behind the scenes, attempting to control all potential eventualities?

Nobody knows?

I can't help but ask myself, do I believe in fate? What role do I play? My response is, the world is bigger than I am.

Terrified, I press on.

I decide to sort through some of this hard core matter in the lab to see if I can find clues that will shed light on the present catastrophe. Entering now an even more perilous territory covered with sharp metal objects and other slippery cutting edge materials, I'm hyper careful not to fall or slide into anything that would slice like butter through human skin. Hundreds of unanimated robot parts are now even more clearly in evidence, as well as AI paraphernalia with diagrams and schemas for uploading super sensational computer data into what appears, as least as far as I make out, the human brain. I remember how digital proposals for 'deep learning' had been fashionable, not merely for commerce, but with even greater acceleration for human enhancement.

The popular mantras were: "Discover yourself. Digitize a solution for your life. Ride the wave and have a digital transformation. Plug in to acquire excellent personal strategies, and brilliant ultra-ideas. Upload the best files for living out your dreams." The digital generation was proliferating at lighting speed. Marketing made it out to be something like this: "You could be BIG DATA and optimize your life. Just implant one of these fiber filaments into your brain and all will be well." One of the central features in this sort of lure was self-improvement and the competition was fierce for becoming ME.

In addition, security weighed in heavily in this environment, since paranoia increased exponentially and haunted most humans. They longed for security and were willing to do almost anything to obtain and possess it. High tech became an essential and perhaps mandatory element of life on Earth, but once humans were hyper connected, as this lab seemed to indicate, there was potentially no turning back from mass production, where some humans started to become like industrial machines.

As I continue my exploration here, I discover robots with sophisticated built in laser weapons powerful enough to destroy human flesh in the blink of an eye. While all this provides clues as to what kind of things were going on, it doesn't help me understand where all the other humans, techno-sapiens, and robots had disappeared to. Perhaps, they were all dead; destroyed, blasted into lifeless parts. Or maybe there had been a mass exodus to another planet.

Who knows?

I tell myself I need to move on, so I do. I'm glad to leave this grotesque lab type setting, since it deepens my anxiety and bewilderment. Further along up the tortuous street, I notice the remains of what must have been an ancient castle. Massive fireplaces are free standing and the bars of what looked like dungeons are still intact. Parts of the high ceilings and the gigantic rooms with weaponry and war gear are also in evidence.

To which historical period all this referred to is a mystery to me. Dates, occupants, and rulers are open questions. Perhaps I'm in some sort of old museum preserved for a contemporary generation and that offered a sense of time, space, and life on Earth in days past. Seems like a spooky place. When I turn to leave, I see a strange macabre creature of some kind. It's translucent, yet at the same time wildly colorful in the light, sort of floating or dancing in the air.

Absolutely striking!

My mind/body experience suddenly careens all over the place, as if I'm losing control. Far out. The powerful invasion and infusion of these colors is blowing me away. After some time, who knows how long, I snap back. Then, the captivating creature appears as if it wants to speak, but I can only hear a whimper. Is this the guardian or ghost of the castle, and am I invading its space? I have no idea what this thing is and whether it's out to harm or help me. Eventually, embracing suspicion over trust, even though I've got nothing to lose (or do I?), I look for the fastest escape route. After a quick scanning of the various options, I choose one, but it leads to a dead end. The thing is still hovering in the air.

Where next?

Trying another possibility, I find myself in a smoke-filled chamber. No way forward here. I back up, step by step being careful not to fall. My last resort is to head through a huge heavy double doorway frame and over a wobbly plank, and then I am out of the castle. The floating creature or whatever it is, does not follow me.

Phew! Terrified, I press on.

After this strange encounter, I wander off towards the left and continue up the street. While walking, I can't help but reflect on what just happened. Trust and suspicion vied for control. But what might that look like? Maybe my genes, body, brain, environment, drive me in the direction of these two center pieces of being human. Suspicion had grown and became a mighty force in my life, especially as things on Earth deteriorated. Politics, churches, institutions, and corporations did not deserve to be trusted. I realized that. But trust is still critical to who I am. I'd wager it actually pervades human essence and identity and is even more monumental than suspicion. After all, I have to trust my suspicion, as I just did in the castle. Whether that was the right choice or not, I'll probably never know.

As I go on up the street, it is getting hotter and hotter, and harder to breathe. Climate chaos had done horrible damage and even more so now. It appears to be one of the causes of the devastation that surrounds me. Glaciers had melted, arctic ice all but gone, the cryosphere rundown, and the weather configurations now completely erratic.

What bizarre and extreme patterns would develop?

It could be totally freezing, as it had been earlier, or exceedingly hot as it is now. It all happened so fast; kind of like a hyper speeded up scene on a screen. You lose your balance, your equilibrium is distorted, and you're overwhelmed by the pace of it all.

But, what is it? What's going on?

Somewhat dizzy and beginning to sweat, I turn into a dilapidated house searching for shade and clues. Entering this space, I begin to cool off a little. I see what appears to be a large diamond shaped object, or is it a subject, that illuminates with a deep, yet transparent purple color. Streams of bright yellow lines like interconnected webs are zooming around inside. It's almost as if they are dynamic energy sequences vibrantly pulsating in a confined space – maybe a digital brain of some kind? It can't, I think, be powered by electricity because there is none. Does it have its own source? Perhaps that's an option, or is something outside of it making it operate? Is it a control center? Can this thing be a result of some kind of eco-engineering, cosmic liaison, or created by techno-advanced beings of some sort?

Who knows?

This late in human evolution it could be any of these, or none. Beyond me. At any rate, I'm mesmerized and feel myself being drawn into a sort of hypnotic state, when all of a sudden, this 'thing' explodes into sparks that start flying all over the place. I cover my face, turn, and dive to the ground trying to protect myself from the shards of energy that are spewed out.

Wow, all I can say is Wow!

What a mega powerful blow-up from something so small. During this episode, I can hear eerie sounds like a screeching or shrieking, as if someone is howling in pain. Not sure how long I stay lying there, but gradually it stops and then is silent. I slowly gain enough courage to get up and look around. There are streams of bright yellow tissue like substance smattered all over the cracked walls and torn floor. I stumble out of the house and back into the street. What has just happened? Did this thing blow-up on its own accord? Did something or someone else detonate it? No explanations come to mind about this strange experience, and I decide to move on.

At this stage, the heat is so overwhelming that, you know how it is, I just want to chill. But I venture into what was probably once upon a time an official admin building of some kind. The windows are shattered, tables, chairs, and file cabinets upended and smashed, and there is paper all over the place, though it is cooler in here. I roam around for a while, how long I'll never know. I find lots of old hard copy documents/records in this place, which is mind boggling. Nothing now is like it was previously from what I can tell by looking at maps, documents, and measurements, when those sorts of things used to be dated and archived. I glance through a register of ancient births, deaths, and burials in the midst of the clutter and recall reading somewhere that apparently early humans may have buried their dead to protect the remaining living from predators. If this was the case, burial was not necessarily some expression of the sacred, but a prerogative for survival. Of course, there might be a dimension of both and more to these ancient burial rites and their enduring traditions, as the evolutionary niche unfolded and interwove neuro, biological, sociological, and cultural diversity into its onward march. Humans and some of their predecessors could have had some very unique and revered practices regarding the dead. At any rate, as intriguing as all this is, I'm not getting any further in my search by examining old records, so I head back out to the streets. It is cooling off, which is a relief, even though I fear it will become glacially cold again in no time. A powerful wind is blowing and the ever present stench seems to increase with it.

Terrified, I press on.

I decide to leave what probably used to be a main street, and turned right into a somewhat smaller, yet equally devastated cross street. Crawling on all fours over the wreckage, I look up and see a line of musical notes floating above me, and then I hear a chaotic fusion of what I think might be voices and instruments. The sounds are both comforting and disturbing, but as they go on the latter takes over. I'm perplexed and start to feel anxious. It is an effort, even a struggle to make anything out of this frenzied concoction. At first, I thought I detected human voices, but now I'm not so sure. Where is this coming from? Some super tech symphonic mastery from aliens? Some centralized power structure that is playing around with the last earthling? Or maybe a message pertaining to my situation? If so, how am I supposed to decipher it, since there are no human sounds or words? This is something like a garbled jamming, I think to myself, my brain is being jammed with sounds that are bewilderingly unfamiliar. But to what end? After some time, who knows how long, the noise is having a dark impact on me. I feel strong paranoia coming on and think maybe I'm undergoing some form of brainwashing. I decide I need to get out of here and escape this vertiginous cacophony that is now driving me crazy. I make my way out of the street as fast as I can, running over piles of broken glass and other sharp matter. I have to be careful, but I make it back alright and then I notice that the sound has stopped. Cool! But I'm spent. This weird experience has taken its toll on both my psycho/physical levels, and I'm worn out. I catch my breath, gather myself, and reflect on what just happened, for how long I'll probably never know.

In the unnerving silence, my thoughts take off again. The human race and its search for the extra-ordinary, always experimenting with the unknown, had become incessant and had possibly gone too far. The mundane or normal was uninteresting and boring. The goal of recent decades was to escape into the 'realm of the transcendent;' with headlines like this: Take a plunge into the mysterious. Break free from all restraints. Disappear and reappear. Streamline a drug concoction and test the limits of life to death and back. Move to the moon, Venus, Mars, or another planet. Be a techno-galactic adventurer.

Seek to *live* forever!

Numerous possibilities were opened up, including outer space travel and 'getting wired' into another sphere. Strikingly, humans were enamored with the idea of surpassing being human. But in contrast, humans were, so far as I know, the only ones in evolutionary emergence to make the imaginary material. A pretty remarkable trait. And once thought to be special. That is, humans previously were not likely to be interested in escaping humanness, but in embracing it. I think encountering the infinite mystery of another human being used to be a sacramental invitation and a sacred adventure towards convergence. This coming alongside or together phenomenon took place at different levels; it was never nothing or everything. To be unaffected by or irredeemably lost in an-other is an expression of inappropriate selfhood. But it seems like humans, were always to be intensely touched by their engagements, while remaining themselves. What happened to humans?

Contemplating these perspectives has left me discouraged and tired. Not that I'm giving up my search for what is going on and why I appear to be here alone, but I'm not getting anywhere at the moment and need some rest and a change of direction for a spell.

Stumbling along in a sort of daze, not paying too much attention to where my feet are leading me, I end up in an alleyway. I'm fearful about this because of what just happened, but I take the risk and go ahead anyway. I have to climb over blocks of concrete and avoid fallen electrical wires that set off weak, but dangerous sparks of dying energy. The wind is even stronger now and the freezing cold has returned. After what seems like days and nights of wandering around, I'm in desperate need of shelter. Going into one of the few partially intact buildings, I realize I'm entering what used to be a vast art museum and library. Books are scattered about. Wow, so many books. Look at them all. Reading one is tempting, but maybe later. Shelves and tables are toppled over. Paintings are lying in the remains. I think to myself, so much for the hallmarks of beauty and learning. They're shattered.

Terrified, I press on.

It's a relief to be out of the wind and somewhat protected from the bitter cold. Step by step I prudently make my way into the library. What a glorious place for books this library once was. The immensity of it, palatial in grandeur, is impressive. Stained glass windows now broken to pieces lie here and there, with brilliant deep reds, blues, greens, and yellows still visible. These must have offered a stunning atmosphere within which to read, reflect, research, and imagine. Proceeding warily through the wreckage, I have to duck to avoid beams perilously hanging from an old oval shaped ceiling. There is enough of it still intact to see that this astonishing work of craftsperson ship is magical. Extraordinary! In another part of the library, some debris falls with a massive thud, and I back away.

Struck by this dramatic scene of ruin and beauty, I begin to weep uncontrollably. Overcome by the emotion of my own state of being and shrouded in the mists of time, I have a strange and strong sense of loss. For some reason, this feeling of desperation drives me further into the recesses of my own life, and leads me into probing the joys and sorrows of my existence. In a flash, images of people I knew come to me: my family; Robert, a friend, who was a promising opera conductor and gave it all up to become a monk; Julie, a friend I went to school with, who ended up married to a plumber and never cheated on him; Winston, an artist; Emily, a ballet dancer; Vera, the beautician; Mark, the philosopher.

What uncanny and wonderful encounters!

These people and a flood of other images seep into what feels like every nerve ending in my body, leaving me somewhat electrified. I can no longer distinguish my feelings then from my feelings now. Sensations of the past and present seem to fuse. This surge drains me and zaps my already feeble strength. Bemused, I find myself drifting further away into the past.

I end up lured back to those long lost years of what happened in San Francisco once upon a time. Young people were then flooding into SF from all over the world during the ancient days of the 1960's. Surprisingly, Haight Street, a previously calm and familial neighborhood, was the new place to be at that time. The majority of the old residents moved out, to make room for the influx. In just a couple of years the air was electric with change, shredding the traditional ways and embracing innovative new ones. Real freaks and fake freaks, charlatans and genuine seekers, roamed the street looking for who knew what. Maybe it was love, friendship, and community. These thoughts evoke others. Thousands and thousands of LSD trips took place in SF during this period of mind-expanding research. Before they became "trendy," psychedelics were an experimental quest. Experiencing stunningly colorful hallucinations of melting trees and flowing grass, those 'dropping' acid were also looking for deep meaning and an intense encounter with a "possible world."

What and who was real?

How could you connect with *life* in the midst of *death*? Did God exist?

Was anything true?

Were ideas relevant to ponder and to seek to understand? Did anything matter?

It was a momentous time. Huge questions and challenges like these were circulating around in music, art, and literature. Culture was rocking as it had perhaps, never done before. So, you might say this was a quest for ideology and utopia rolled into one. As time went on there was free food, lodging, drugs, and medical care. Those who had shared with those who hadn't. Communal living started to expand and quickly became a new lifestyle.

The mantra of 'invitation' spread like wildfire.

But something else was brewing in the wider context. Massive racial issues came to the surface, presenting dreadful stories of injustice, of hatred and the bigotry of 'white' culture and society. Non-white people, who had been oppressed for generations, were beginning to break free, though thousands were mowed down, a repetition of the horror and devastation of previous racial battles. The cruelty and deceit of white power was like an evil wand in the hands of dishonest maniacs. Political corruption was rampant and trust in tradition was fading fast, if it still existed at all. A wide social upheaval was bursting at the seams, and was long overdue. Back in SF, strange days were upon the city, and society was moving in new directions almost in spite of itself and threatened the status quo.

Not only were people in the streets about racial oppression, but marches against American involvement in Vietnam were prevalent at this time. The awful and horrific events at Kent State, Ohio, where protesting students were killed, rang out around the nation and world. The country as a whole and the different generations were probably never as divided as they were then. Clashes over free speech and the right to assemble and protest were frequently brought to court. Many were swept up into these ground-breaking moments, reading Nietzsche, Hegel, Sartre, Camus, and others.

Revolution was in the air.

Trying to make sense of life was like swimming upstream in a raging river. There was so much to think through and be challenged by. LSD continued to explode in popularity and it seemed like half of SF was high. As the exploration went on, there were good acid trips and bad ones. Sometimes, after ingesting a sugar cube laced with liquid LSD, a scene of bliss arose, making visible an unseen harmony in the world. Solace, shelter, and peace were all so close, so damn close. But other times, a trip could raise fears of being lost forever. The pulsating aura of never, ever, coming down to the ground, whatever in actuality that really was, could shred the 'I' into many pieces, leaving it so fragmented that it would not be able to be put back together again. This threat made it a challenge to keep in step with the mantra of,

"Turn On, Tune In, Drop Out."

Risk, experiment, and freedom were what it was all about. And why not? Who knew where they would end up? Some became heroin addicts, others lost their minds, others graduated from University with PhD's, and others opened a business. The diversity was striking. There were so many, many people tripping and going off in a mixture of directions with vastly different results. Some of which brought sadness, but others joy. Bewildering and perplexing. But wasn't it always like this? Long invigorating conversations and profound questions on these and other tensions in life were surely in evidence. Asking questions was a norm, not an exception. Questions; there were so many questions. And it seemed like so few answers.

Outlandish and interesting ideas were taking hold and leading SF and many other locations in a far more radical direction than what had preceded it. This scene no doubt became an international phenomenon, but SF remained at the heart of it all.

Day and nights spent hanging out in the Park, listening to live music, heightened a sense of community and well-being. Gatherings like this tended to promote a new way of approaching life. Somehow the music played a highly significant role in the community and vice versa. They were like partners in love and protest, care, and rebellion. These were the days where musicians were just part of everything else that was going on.

And the music of the times was a fantastic blur of styles, including anything from folk, to blues, to jazz. Poets, singers, and songwriters were becoming more well-known with what were taken by many to be versions of anti-establishment songs. While there was an ideological continuity, the sound nevertheless began to evolve and develop. The acoustic, for example, became less evident and amplifiers gained ground.

Then the electric music scene broke through with musicians like, Jimi Hendrix and *Purple Haze*, Jim Morrison / the Doors and *The End* and hundreds of others. But many SF bands, including the Grateful Dead, Quicksilver Messenger Service, Jefferson Airplane, and Big Brother & the Holding Company had their own unique sounds, much to their credit.

The lonely and lost found a home in SF. Leaving the Park and entering Haight Street no one could help but recognize what a legendary phenomenon this part of the city had become. Busloads of tourists, staying safely inside their buses, constantly cruised up the Street. These people, from who knows where, gawked at the women with no bras, the men with long hair, and the psychedelically painted houses and cars.

Plenty of onlookers saw this no doubt as a ride through a kind of zoo, observing and photographing unusual looking "animals" in their habitat. These folks didn't have a clue to what was really going on here. Not a radical or inquisitive bone in their body.

Things were changing during these renowned times. Hope for a new age was everywhere. But in the end it was over in a blink of an eye, and actually not a whole lot really changed. I wondered what happened to the activists and protesters, as this vision of a new culture began to disappear. Seemed like everyone and everything gradually just merged into the system and it all lost momentum, if there really was any there to begin with. When protest and opposition are packaged and sold as products they lose their raison d'être. Unfortunately, this unusual period waned, having made some progress, but not enough, and it was now only to be relived in memories and stories of the faded past. Then things deteriorated quickly, with increasing social, ecological, and economic corruption endangering the planet and humanity. My voyage into the past through thoughts and memories seems to have spanned hours, and it takes a while before I'm able to salvage a slender thread of composure.

But it's difficult to tell. What is time anyway? Does it matter, or how does it matter?

I believe that it was Saint Augustine who wrote somewhere that he knew very well what time was until someone asked him. Well, I can relate to that. Not that there is anyone asking me, but I just don't know.

Mysterious concept, isn't it?

Past, present, and future, sun, moon, stars, and planets all fit together in some manner, yet the great paradox of time escapes me. I recall that both the momentous work of Marcel Proust in *Remembrance of Things Past* and the delightful, though ominous story by Thomas Mann in *The Magic Mountain*, had wrestled with the prodigious enigma of time, perhaps to no avail. Yet these narratives remain fascinating as they sought to capture a piece of the unexplainable and to recount a sliver of the human story in the dimension(s) of time.

Emerging from this emotive and reflective state, or whatever it was, I gradually remember what I had been intending to do. Here before me is a library and a world of books; oh, yes, I say to myself, the books. Re-entering the library, in spite of its precarious condition, is inspiring. I'm surrounded by a vast array of volumes and it is as if they are speaking out to me, throbbing with meaning. My previous thought patterns return. I was tempted to pick a book and read. That's it. I take a step forward over more wreckage, and then a striking set of hues, blue, red, and orange, appear through the cracked stained glass. These dense colors are thickly textured and soothing to the eyes. It spurs me on to what's next.

But what should that be? What do I do now? Rest? Bury myself in a corner and read? Wander through the ruined art museum and look at the works left clinging to fractured walls or lying on the floor?

Art had such a long history from cave paintings to canvases and was surely one of the revealing traits of primates something like me, marked by an abundance of imagination and creativity. Art? Books? I've always had difficulty in making decisions, and the hazardous circumstances that I'm in have not changed that. I eventually decide to settle down in spite of my angst, and start flipping through one book and then another.

Many of these are damaged or beyond repair, yet others have escaped the threat of non-existence and are more or less intact. Soon I find myself beginning to read, instead of just flitting through the pages, and I gradually become immersed in a story that draws me into another world.

While I had often assumed that a story was just a story, I find myself getting lost in narrated time. I had heard about clock time fading away, but while I sit reading it seems to have now completely disappeared. During this moment, or perhaps it is hours, the ever present and intense sense of fear within me subsides some, and I'm able to think other thoughts.

The first story I read is set in Paris. The lavish descriptions of the city's beauty are remarkable. Images in words give wings to imagination. Soaring over the Eiffel Tower, floating through the Louvre, praying in Notre Dame, and gliding along the Champs Elysees are breathtaking. These illustrious monuments and landmarks are nothing short of a magnificent tribute to the creative efforts of humanity. All this, combined with the atmosphere of theaters, cafés, gourmet restaurants, and the gently flowing river Seine, made Paris unique and exceptional. "Parisesque." I put the book down and savor the imagery it evokes: but then recall my present environment of desolation and emptiness. This drives me to quickly get back into the story.

The main character in the book is a prostitute, who calls herself Aita. Aita has a fascinating array of clients. A butcher, a lawyer, an architect, a writer, and a historian, are among those who pay regular visits to the attractive lady. When not practicing her trade, Aita spends much of her time making contacts with script writers, directors, and others in the movie guild. Her dream is to eventually become an actress. She has tremendous talent and through her hard work she begins to be recognized and is offered more and more roles in films. Parts are small at first, but over time she becomes a lead actress. In her latest film, Aita deals with virtue lost and re-gained, a grueling tale of love and deceit filmed in the South of France. Ironically, having left prostitution behind, many of the questions and issues developed in the scenario connect with her own life. And this turns out to be a marvel. As the film winds its way to conclusion, the character begins to embrace new directions for herself: Rooting out self/other deception she opens up to credible trust. And in playing the role, Aita learns that she too can embrace them. This is a sort of redemption theme in a major key, and with this the story ends. Nervously, I close the book. There is much to take from this narrative and I find myself enriched, not least with the notion of a transformative orientation.

In leaving the world of Aita, Paris, and the lessons of life from the story/film, I'm once again struck by fear. Alarmed. Scrambling to my feet, somewhat bedazzled by the contrast between the story I had been immersed in and what is apparently real, my hunger and thirst overtake my fear and become more pressing. I'm starving and dehydrated. I have had nothing, for how long I'll never know, to eat or drink since my crackers and water. I need to find something soon. I long for the taste of something satisfying, comforting, and nourishing. What I'd give for a hot meal, a glass of robust red wine, a strong coffee, a piece of rich dark chocolate, such full bodied flavors, textures, and smells. This brings to mind a vague memory of a celebration some decades ago where, if I recall accurately, I had a delicious lunch. I wonder if it will ever be possible to savor such tastes and aromas after all this. Unfortunately, they are no longer available in my present life.

Compelled to venture out of the library in search of material sustenance, my senses drive me east in hope of finding a house or store with something left that isn't destroyed or spoiled. Being careful not to lose my bearings, and in order to find my way back to what has become a home base of sorts, I leave behind me markers of tattered and charred red cloth held down by rocks and pieces of concrete that are strewn around in various locations. I'm freezing. My face tingling with cold, I hurry along, hands in pockets trying to get warm. The thought of food and drink though is like an imaginative impulse that makes me realize that I cannot live on imagination and books alone.

I need physical nourishment badly.

I search through cupboards in empty demolished houses, under fallen shelves in abandoned caved in supermarkets, and behind counters in crumbling vacant bakeries. What happened to the stocks of non-perishable food and water? Ransacked? Destroyed? Sold out and never replenished? I know supply chains had become notoriously dysfunctional and perhaps they had broken down totally as the economy worsened. Not being able to find any cans or dried food makes me wonder how long ago production has ceased. After spending serious energy hunting around for provisions of any kind, and being close to exhaustion, I finally come upon a carton of stale, but edible wafers, and then a fountain of water gushing from a broken underground main – wafers and water.

This reminds me of the old stories of prisoners having to survive on rudimentary elements. How did they ever make it? Feeling a bit like a prisoner myself, the wafers and water are not much, but they are something precious in a world of nothing. After eating my fill and drinking plenty of water, I rest for a spell.

Later, I find my way back to the library, following the rags I left to mark the way home. And I return to the world of books. The rampant fear of solitude still hangs over me like Damocles' sword and the sensation of being towards death is as thick as a dense and billowing fog sweeping through the old San Francisco Golden Gate.

Is this what it has all come down to? Quenching hunger and thirst? A roll of the dice where anything can happen? But what about all the symbols of life, beauty, and love?

Who knows, I keep repeating – who knows?

This recurring question has become a sort of unrelenting mantra, embedded within my subterranean memory banks and which keeps resurfacing over and over and over again.

And then I swear I see a black cat. You know how you can catch a glimpse, a flicker of something out of the corner of your eye. Scrambling as fast as I can through the dust and ruins, I attempt to get a better view. Maybe after all, it is a rat. Or, it is neither a cat nor a rat, but a hallucination of one or the other? No, I swear it is a cat, but whatever I think I see or really did see, vanishes and is no longer there. As far as I can tell, I'm still alone in the emerging darkness.

Since the light now is rapidly disappearing, there is no time left to engage another book. Hopefully, I will now be able to sleep, even though it's still freezing and gloomy. I look for and find some cardboard, and spread it under me and over me trusting that what I had seen the homeless do, desperately trying to get a shard of warmth, might possibly work for me. I'm sheltered from the wind by some of the still standing library walls, but there is so much open space on both sides and above me that I figure all this wrapping up is a waste of time. But lo and behold I doze off and eventually experience trickles of body heat that allows me to be somewhat comfortable. I must have then actually fallen into a deeper sleep.

When I awake, the stench of dead flesh or whatever it is remains pungent. I'm still freezing, weak, and breathing with difficulty. I decide to get up and move around. At that moment, I remember having some interesting, though convoluted dreams. Everything is a bit vague and opaque, but at least I recognize some distinction between a sleeping and a waking mode and that gives me courage. For what, I still don't know. It is an intense sensation, whatever it's worth. The dreams though took me through several levels and into various atmospheres, and somehow brings out into the open a number of bits and pieces of time gone by. What a remarkable state the dream state is, and in many ways similar to imagination in the sense of being in two places at the same time – here and there.

In the first dream, women were taking to the streets of Rome, Geneva, New York, and Sydney to protest against the injustices that had smothered them for so many centuries. From the time of the earliest philosophers and for centuries after, women were portrayed and treated as inferior to men. Even when science began to show this was not the case, men found ways around the data to maintain the old traditional views that kept women in check. Wombs were simply storage containers for men's seed and breasts feeding centers for children, and women added nothing substantial to pro-creation. Such ignorant views held prominence for centuries and centuries until the knowledge against them became so overwhelming it could no longer be side-stepped: women were in every sense as essential as men, if not more so. They gained a well-deserved voice after having been silenced for so very long. No more false guilt and shame, no rigorous diet regimes, or beauty myths that kept females in line with male controlled standards and under the authority of advertisers and plastic surgeons. These ladies, now free, sought political, institutional, and aesthetic power and brought greater measures of equality and fairness into the modern world, which had rarely operated this way before.

My next dream led me into a room - space where ghost-like figures were arguing about destructive relationships. Their voices were faint and garbled, yet I could just make out what was being said. The whole scenario seemed as if it was a tragic Shakespearean play or a novel by Sartre. Betrayal and deception led to broken trust and a high degree of suspicion between the characters. Who lied? Who cheated? It was hard to tell who had not been wronged and who had. The back and forth bantering created an emotionally charged and tense atmosphere. There was rivalry, jealousy, and corruption. One accused the other and vice-versa. The cacophony of disputes seemed to go on and on without resolution.

When this scene abruptly faded, it was replaced by another. Amazing vistas stretching out for what seemed like kilometers. Magnificent green and brown trees with massive foliage lined the dirt roads, flowers dropped from the rainbow colored sky, and deep black rivers violently plunged and careened off gigantic boulders to who knows where? And then I saw white cars that had been trashed and green garbage cans lying all over the place.

Then two women appeared surrounded by a clan of elves.

One tall, almost like a giant, with striking coal black hair and blazing garments. The other looked like a pathfinder with a bow and arrows, her skin was like silver and she had a mosaic tattoo on her leg. They were valiant warriors – "gladiatoresses" and honored and respected by their subjects. Both carried a sword and knife. Their icy blue eyes scanned the landscape like a hawk searching for prey. They moved quickly as if tragedy was about to strike. I got the distinct impression they were forcibly holding back the rushing black waters of a powerful vortex that threatened the inhabitants. All of a sudden, down and down they went, but in so doing they diverted the deluge and saved their clan.

Sacrificially - lost.

Great sorrow overcame the tribe and there was uncontrollable weeping. It seemed as if it must have been this strong emotion of grief that startled me from my dream state into awakening. Who knows? Waking up is sort of like fighting your way through cobwebs and wondering what it was that caused you to finally break through the mist. Dreams... .?

After these dreams slip away I'm more fully awake, or at least I think I am. I wander around in the library. Then I decide to do some jumping jacks and quick cardio exercises to warm up a bit, and I'm finally able to settle down to read another book.

As I gaze at the volumes surrounding me, I can't help but reflect on all the creative ideas they contain and that contributed to protecting humanity and its environment over the course of time. Liberty, equality, justice, and hope were mantras that circulated through the centuries. Save the disenfranchised, save the stranger, save the whales, save the tigers, save the forests, save the world.

But such wise and wonderful proposals must have been ignored, as human hubris continued its march towards what it believed was progress, becoming master of it all. It's likely that some had purposefully promoted deceptions for monetary gain with horrific implications for the planet. This sort of destructive game playing could not go on forever.

It couldn't. It didn't. I guess.

Had it really come to being a post-truth/post-trust culture with so many fake promises and what appeared as the downright betrayal of humanity and Earth for power and profit? Probably! But with my memories and imagination running wild, I still can't put my finger on what's really going on here.

Shaking myself, which is becoming rather a habit lately, jolts me back to the present and my longing to read. After brushing the dust and rubble off one book, I notice it's a publication of poems. I love poetry, and had even written a bit when younger. I then think about something. Poetry so often tells a story. Poets create and put together words and metaphors that spike imagination and stretch it to the limits; they create worlds I can live in. These reflections whet my appetite. I cherish the making of pictures with words, so I open the ancient book and find a poem written by Samuel Taylor Coleridge.

He wrote *What is Life?* around 1805.

Resembles Life what once was held of Light,
Too ample in itself for human sight?
An absolute Self—an element ungrounded—
All, that we see, all colours of all shade

By encroach of darkness made?—
Is very life by consciousness unbounded?
And all the thoughts, pains, joys of mortal breath,
A war-embrace of wrestling Life and Death?

For me, it is as if this had been written today. These words resonate in a way they never could have before. When I reflect on where I am now, I sense a real connection. The struggle of Life and Death. Does consciousness make what is? Seems like it.

But oh, light and darkness, are such wonderful metaphors that lead to a variety of images and musings. Illuminating the path, a darkening mood, the visible and the hidden, hope and fear, joy and sorrow, all have uncanny associations with seeing in the light and not seeing in the dark. Any answer though to "what is life" depends in some sense on who I am.

Do I have limits or no grounding? And at this point, who cares? Somehow, even in the midst of my present debacle, I guess I do.

Why?

But seriously, I could be floating untethered in the sky or freezing my butt off in a library. And life itself then would be nothing other than a bold mystery that compels me again and again to explore the contours of a lost world – a world seemingly without end, or is it?

Flipping on through this book, other lines from another poem stand out. It was written by a contemporary of Coleridge, William Wordsworth, and is entitled *The Prelude*, the version of 1805 Book 8.

Such was my new condition, as at large
Has been set forth; yet here the vulgar light
Of present actual superficial life,
Gleaming through colouring of other times,
Old usages and local privilege,
Thereby was softened, almost solemnized,
And rendered apt and pleasing to the view;
This notwithstanding, being brought more near
As I was now, to guilt and wretchedness,
I trembled, thought of human life at times
With an indefinite terror and dismay
Such as the storms and angry elements
Had bred in me, but gloomier far, a dim
Analogy to uproar and misrule,
Disquiet, danger, and obscurity.

Then these lines from *The Prelude*, Book 10, where Wordsworth expresses the detrimental effects of rationalism:

Thus I fared,
Dragging all passions, notions, shapes of faith,
Like culprits of the bar, suspiciously
Calling the mind to establish in plain day
Her titles and her honours, now believing,
Now disbelieving, endlessly perplexed
With impulse, motive, right and wrong, the ground
Of moral obligation, what the rule
And what the sanction, till, demanding proof,
And seeing in everything, I lost

All feeling of conviction, and, in fine,
Sick, wearied out with contrarieties,
Yielded up moral questions in despair

The flow of thoughts and words is spellbinding. It brings to the surface such emotions as uncertainty, dismay, anger, and fear. I am amazed how fully I resonate with a poem and a poet from so long ago. But then sort of lost in a sea of reflection on these words tends to dampen my passions and numb my sensitivities, so that aligned with the poem there is a seeming obscurity lurking over my existence, which leaves me suspicious and baffled. Flickering around inside like a short circuit, I'm gradually edging towards despair where "vulgar light" and "superficial life" weigh heavily upon me. I have to confess to myself, I'm hyper-vulnerable. Wordsworth's art is so close to being appallingly sublime: life giving and life haunting at the same time. I decide that this poetry in all its grandeur is too revealing and too challenging for me at the moment, and that perhaps I can consume, and be consumed by more, a little later. Right now though, I think, I'm going to venture out to change things up, and see if there are any signs of life around, and to hopefully find something to eat and drink.

Terrified, I press on.

Leaving the library, the pungent odor still prevalent and growing stronger, continues to make me quasi nauseous and my fight against the unceasing cold is an ongoing labor. The sky is misty greyish with a few dark clouds in the backdrop, and I expect it to rain. It doesn't. Should I change my itinerary this time? I deliberate. Head off in another direction in hopes of finding sustenance that might turn out better than last time? Or do I follow the path I had previously traveled?

I decide on a new direction.

I am again struck by the vast emptiness that surrounds me. The eerie silence screams out at me. It is truly deafening. Hands in pockets, shoulders hunched up, I start walking. This time I have ash white strips of cloth to mark the way for my return. When I look to the left, I see the graffiti etched on some of the old walls, but the previously vivid colors are now tarnished with dusty grime that makes it difficult to decipher. My progress is slow today, but a hundred meters ahead the road looks a bit clearer. Clambering over one obstacle and then another, and side-stepping more chunks of concrete, I finally arrive at a space where it is easier to move without having to fight for each step through this tormented landscape.

Suddenly, something like a glaring piece of bronze streaks through the clouds and catches my eye. I recoil. Faced with the decision of either to hide or to stay put, I choose the latter. Just as I do, there is an explosion producing a kaleidoscope of colors, which then disappears, sort of like fireworks used to do. One part of my human brain demands to make sense of the phenomenon. It seems as if the intricate and highly complex mind of a human always wants to explain everything. Is there a "who" or a "what" to discover and understand? Perplexed, I turn away and pursue my quest for food and drink.

Foraging around in dilapidated buildings full of dust and piles of bricks and mortar takes a lot of energy, which I'm extremely low on, but this time it eventually pays off. I come upon a treasure: a closed jar of honey that isn't spoiled. This is precious stuff and will go well with the stale wafers I have left. As I leave the ramshackle mess of a house and turn to go back, I notice forty meters or so off in the opposite direction a broken pipe spurting water. Looks promising. I have to go check this out. I'm desperate for a drink.

I think to myself, if I could only find a container I'd be able to carry some water with me. It would be helpful to have a supply, even a small one. To my good fortune, I find a metallic object that is big enough to half fill and still be able to carry. I figure this successful exploration is enough for today, and that I should now find my way back to the library. Water, wafers, and honey means my life is improving. After arriving "home," I eat and drink what in some ways seems, at least typologically, a sacred meal. Dazed by fatigue, I then have a rather unconfident and somewhat restless sleep, but at least it gives me a partial respite for what is to come next.

I'm awakened by a loud crash that frightens me. I turn and notice debris falling off a wall. At first I think, someone is maybe in the library, but to my disappointment, no one appears. After getting up and doing my usual warm-ups, I gradually decide that it's time to explore other parts of the library. I'm intrigued in finding out more about the books on the other side of this vast space. As the old literary theorists used to quip, "It's possible to live because it's possible to read," though they probably thought this does not necessarily commit one to an official or particular view of reality. And who knows, they're probably right. Books, books, and more books. What to make of them all? But, I wonder, does reading and living have a deeper connection that has somehow previously escaped me.

Wending my way through the clutter, I begin to feel ever more unsettled. I think I may even collapse. Give up. Throw it in.

What has happened to put me in this condition?

Is it that nothing has changed as time dredges on from one day to the next? On and on it seems to go. Day and night – night and day. The cold and heat, the stench, the hunger and thirst are devastating enough, but the plague of being alone is the most staggering. I stop and sit on a mass of debris. Eventually, who knows how long it took, I recover my composure and start off again.

Then, it occurs to me, all this is maybe something like being one of those characters in an existential novel where the only real choice is to commit suicide or not. Everything else is secondary. But, as in some of these stories instead of committing suicide, viewed as the ultimate cop out, I too am to live life, and embrace it as an act of resistance, in spite of it being utterly meaningless. One might say, those who "chose" this path were the heroes and heroines of old. They took the world for what it was – absurd – but refused to be lulled into complacency or daunted by death, and faced the overwhelming odds against survival with courage and lucidity bringing some meaning to their lives in doing it. Ha! I could be a real life illustration from a novel. Yet, I have no idea if these meanderings are, in the existentialists' terms, a *remedy* or a *poison*. I imagine the former. What is important is to connect to the *moment,* move on to the next and see what happens. Keep rolling the proverbial stone up the mountain, only to have it fall back down, and finding myself along-side Sisyphus in becoming an Underworld laborer. The existentialists were such thought provoking writers.

I now continue my journey to the other side of the library. As it turns out, it is a laborious trip indeed. I stumble over something and fall almost hitting my head on a jagged edge of a broken stained glass window, I run into a piece of robust wooden bookcase with my shoulder, I bump my knee against a block of concrete, but in spite of all this, I escape serious injury, with only minor scrapes and cuts. Strangely, life for me isn't getting any simpler, only more complex.

When I finally make my way over to this new location, I decide to sort through the books strewn all over the place and put the undamaged ones into piles. This will make it easier to go through some of them and find out, at least partially, what is here.

In addition to this task, I shove rubble off what looks like and indeed turns out to be a folding desk that has not been crushed, only slightly damaged. The desk will definitely be useable for stacking a small number of books, so that will help. This is what my life is amounting to be all about: a world and worlds of books. My next step is to find a chair. What a simple, yet useful luxury that would be. Clambering around heaps of refuse and pushing mounds of wreckage, I eventually find the remains of something to sit on that looks like it will hold my weight and is close enough to being a chair. I haul first the desk and then the chair back across to where I had come from, this time avoiding the perils that I experienced on my previous journey.

After setting things up, I sit at my desk in the vast library looking out through the collapsed roof and onto the gray sky. There I see what appear to be gold paved streets lined with emerald colored trees. This strikes me as an apocalyptic scene or maybe something similar to an epic in the sky. Crowds of human like beings are strolling along in a flowing fashion. They are visible, yet transparent. Awesome. They beckon me to join them. The psychedelic imagery seems as if it is invitingly spinning towards me, but then quickly moves away.

Should I go? Where? And with whom?

Suddenly, I draw back, feeling increasingly fearful that I am of another world – another sort of creature than they are and therefore I ought to stay put. But, for what? I don't know. Surely, my imagination is overtaxed and there is really nothing there, but my sense that this is taking place is extremely difficult to ignore. In the next moment, it all disappears and this world, my world, is the only thing left. I reflect.

Maybe what we long for isn't ever what is.

After this breathtaking, yet weird experience, I choose to read some more poetry. From *The Prelude*, 1805, Book 6 (525-537):

Imagination! lifting up itself
Before the eye and progress of my Song
Like an unfather'd vapour; here that Power,
In all the might of its endowments, came
Athwart me; I was lost in a cloud,
Halted, without a struggle to break through.
And now recovering, to my Soul I say
I recognize thy glory; in such strength
Of usurpation, in such visitings
Of awful promise, when the light of sense
Goes out in flashes that have shewn to us
The invisible world, doth Greatness make abode,
There harbours whether we be young or old.

Wordsworth's words strike a chord. Such beautiful thoughts. So deep, yet so unsettling. Imagination has never been given enough credit, even by poets. While it was a key source of their words, it was not often enough the topic of their poetry, though in this poem Wordsworth surely tips his pen in its favor. Staving off the desire to stay in a poetic world, which is indeed entrancing, but also somewhat perplexing, I now pick up a different kind of book.

This story, probably dating back decades, takes me to a small village high in the mountains. Most of the people that lived here were trying to survive in meagre circumstances. Only a few shacks/huts were fitted out with running water and electricity.

One of the families, the major focus of the story, had five children, which was considered a small to average size family in those days. All five went to a little local school, sometimes trudging through the heavy winter snow on foot in order to get there. The older four were not at all interested in learning about history, geography, languages, and math. This was fine for them, as they had accepted mountain life and were not really interested in studying or going to university, way off somewhere in the city.

The youngest though wanted to study, Anne-Marie adored books, and most of the subjects at school. Her teacher, in those early years, helped broaden her horizons by lending her books on art and music, and she eventually started writing and learned to sing. While her parents and siblings often made fun of Anne-Marie and thought she was wasting her time on irrelevant interests, an assumption that some in the village shared, she remained courageously determined to stick to her path in spite of adversity. This created a good deal of anxiety and as Anne-Marie got older she felt a fair amount of pressure that threatened to throw her off track. Yet, she was unable to give up on her passion, curiosity, and love of books, no matter what. Many claimed that women did not need to be educated and were better off staying at home, but she refused to be defeated, even when facing severe criticism. Her resistance was not only a matter of will, but also a sign of her strength and intelligence. Eventually, her teacher intervened on her behalf and after a prolonged series of discussions with officials and her parents, Anne-Marie was allowed to leave her family and the village to pursue her education.

In the years that followed, she was accepted into the University to study philosophy and was eventually awarded a PhD for a brilliant thesis on the German philosopher Immanuel Kant. She became a professor, an excellent administrator, and a well-known advocate for women's rights at all levels, especially in their access to education. Her tireless efforts and insights gained her tremendous respect and her impact was monumental – a huge turning point for women at the time.

After finishing the book, I lay it down on the desk and think about it, for how long I'll never know. I can't help but reflect on and imagine what Anne-Marie had to go through and overcome. Absolutely incredible. In the story, she had almost everything against her, yet her bravery, determination, and desire was unwavering.

Amazing!

Anne-Marie, so deftly portrayed by the narrator was indeed ahead of her time and paved the way to freedom for many women who read the book and acted upon it.

Stories enliven imagination and acting on imagination can contribute to changing the world. This is such a fabulous story and one that indeed inspires me to carry on, in spite of my own dire straits.

I then think to myself: stories are phenomenal. I love stories. Primates like me have probably always loved stories. Stories seem to be a deeply intertwined part of the whole of who I am, and that's inspiring.

Storytellers!

Navigating the landscapes of stories is a wonder. They're both absorbed into lives and expressed out of them through living in the world of time. Our imaginations appear to have evolved that way, though perhaps with some transcendent contribution. Surely, our evolutionary history, notably the human niche, is vast and tangled with complexity that goes far beyond thought and emotion, yet stories capture our attention and take us into a "possible world," and it turns out that these "possible worlds" are giving me sustenance and courage in my actual one. I guess I wonder about my own stories too. I recognize something special: I not only read stories, but I also tell them. What stories do I tell myself about myself in particular areas of my life, and why? Hmmm?

Somehow, I can't avoid getting caught up in all sorts of questions. They are like – I don't know – impossible to escape. Maybe that's just part of being a primate like me too.

Curiosity, recounting, and searching for answers are part of who I am. So, in the midst of surviving there are a myriad of questions piling up, both from being alive and from reading stories and poetry. During this reflective moment, how long I'm 'in' it I'll never know, I have a strong sense that someone or something is present. This is nothing I can actually see, but in so many past discussions I had argued for the value of physically 'seeing' as the be all and end all of what was real. Yet, it doesn't seem to me now that there is any viable way to the real without the complex risk of deception, whether seen or unseen. Sometimes, I think, I should trust my eyes, sometimes, I suppose, I shouldn't. Or sometimes I should trust imagination without any material visual, and sometimes I shouldn't. This brings me again to that crazy dynamic between trust and suspicion.

Mind blowing how essential that is to everything!

But what, if anything, is in the library with me? I have a glimmer of hope that someone is here, but alas as I search it appears that my 'sense' of presence is an imaginative impulse. Perhaps it is connected to the narratives and poetry I'm reading, and as I'm surrounded by an enormous host of characters and plots from so many books that all have some kind of 'reality,' I wager this beckons me to feel as though someone is here, and I guess that is the case or is it? Surely, I can't say who or what it is. Much too much remains a mystery.

This leads me to further reminiscing. Some scientists had argued that aliens arrived on Earth, but were invisible. These thinkers looked at the uni or multiverse and thought there must be other life somewhere in this vast amount of space and if there was it is likely that it would be interested in coming to Earth. But in its present state, why would any beings come here? Unless of course they came and went, and took everyone with them, and that was part of the explanation for the existing circumstances I find myself in. Maybe aliens would have appreciated humans, but maybe they would have enslaved them.

So, maybe it is an alien with me in the library?

Who knows?

At this point, I'm famished. My wafers and honey need to be replenished. This is the moment, I think, to venture out and try to scrounge up more food and drink. I head off in another direction, so this time I leave white tattered rags to mark my way back. After I have been out of the library for some time, how long I'll never know, I have the distinct impression that I'm being followed. Just like in the library, these feelings of a presence are stunningly intense. Back in the library I didn't see anyone, and I don't see anyone now either. I decide to dart to my left and climb over a large pile of rubble and then hide in an old shell of a building where I can see if someone is coming behind me. I wait and wait. Well, again I don't see anyone. Someone or something could be there, but I am unable to get to a point of knowing one way or the other if that is really the case.

I need to continue my search for food and pull myself together to carry on, even though the impressions and sensations linger. Foraging around in several dilapidated houses and what looks like gutted and collapsed restaurants is unproductive. I stumble on what used to be white pristine fridges and freezers, now smashed or ripped apart and covered with heaps of dirt and soot. Nothing edible here. I then go through a small dark spooky cavern that eventually opens onto another street or what is left of it. Everything is torn up and it is difficult to piece together what goes with what. Fortunately, when I turn to my left I see a bold psychedelic sign hanging from what must have been a storefront. I push the debris away from the battered sign to see if I can make out what it says.

I think it is *Space Rocks.*

Digging around further, I uncover what used to be or at least was something like an 'outer space store.' It appears that this was a place where you could purchase a variety of things, including gear for surviving on another planet. At that moment, I wish I had gloves to protect my hands during these excavations, and think sooner or later I should try to find some. In the meantime, I keep at it, exposing more and more fragments of material that appears other worldly. And then, in the blink of an eye, I discover loads of packages full of various sorts of high octane food that doesn't spoil. This is like striking gold in the ancient old West. All of a sudden, my food resources, which had been meagre to say the least, dramatically change for the better. This is a huge relief and it immediately lowers my stress levels. Wow! Not having enough to survive is a mantra that dominates my life, as it is often survival that beckons me onwards, and now I can let a part of that go. Sure, none of this food will taste like much, but it is made of essential ingredients, which give vitality and nourishment and that's what counts.

As I come out of this focused state, how long it was I'll never know, I notice that I'm getting hot again. I find a ragged bag and start loading the packets of food in it to take back to the library, so I won't have to return to the *Space Rocks* store every day. Once the bag is full, I head out. When I go back through the eerie cavern, I'm confronted with what looks like a shiny multicolored stainless steel wall with phenomenal metallic doors. It is shockingly immense and seems to have appeared out of nowhere. I muse: from stone tools to hyper complex razor sharp technology, primates like me had indeed come of age. Or was this a primate construction? I suppose I should look for some way to open the doors, so I can maybe see what's inside. This freaks me out a bit and I hesitate. I want to think carefully about my next move.

What should I do? What would someone else do? Walk away and head back to the library? Or try to get through the doors?

I'm not getting any better at making decisions. As usual, when I face a difficult choice, I want to explore several possibilities, before actually doing anything. By now it is really hot, so I go under a half collapsed building for shade. Sheltered from the scorching heat, I ponder what to do. It's amazing what a little shade can offer when you're so hot. After wrangling with myself this way and that trying to analyze my options from various angles, I must have dozed off, as I suddenly now wake up from a frighteningly vivid dream. I dreamt that massive plagues had killed hundreds of thousands of people. They came in fast waves and entirely submerged health care systems. The deadly vehemence of these destructive forces was out of control. Humans were under serious threat from the proliferation of untreatable viruses and mega germs that resisted vaccines and antibiotics. In an attempt to ward off contamination, they lined up to receive chip implants in foreheads and arms, if they weren't already connected through a brain Wi-Fi graft. AI was employed to try to figure out a response. This enfleshed technology was used, under the guise of protection and security, as it provided ultra-sophisticated sensors of detection so that it was possible to steer far clear of anyone infected. But at the same time it was also quite invasive and tracked your every move. Fear reigned.

High-tech as safe and sinister? Freedom or tyranny? Good or evil?

But the plagues continued to claim victims and it appeared that nothing could stop them. Skating rinks and stadiums were commissioned for morgues as the bodies piled up until a massive numbers of boats arrived and took people out to be deposed of in the ocean, as it was impossible to deal with all the dead on land.

Awful! Panic set in.

Quarantines were mandated. Millions world-wide were in lockdown. Time was running out. It is in the midst of this dire situation in my dream that I abruptly awake dripping in sweat. Wow! That was scary and I'm sort of trembling, but I recognize again how fragile human life is having lived through several pandemics myself over the decades. I wager that one of these, at some point, might have indeed taken almost everybody out and brought an end to life as it has been known for centuries and thus creating a completely different kind of world, considerably worse than the one in my dream.

Mind blowing!

It takes me some time to compose myself, don't have any idea how long. I stand up and brush myself off. I finally decide I will be adventurous and attempt to open the doors of the brilliantly shining wall, but when I leave my shady spot and turn to head in that direction it has disappeared. Just like that. Gone wall. I'm perplexed. Human primate hard wiring tends to demand complete clarity, resolution, and guarantee when dealing with objects in the world, but each of these requires faith, faith, and faith. Is this what it is all about? Learning to have faith? Did I really see a stainless steel shimmering wall with doors? Who knows? The questionable difference between image and imagination, reality and illusion plagues me and I long to know, know, know, with ultimate and final certainty. Alas, this longing or maybe even this programming in my DNA and brain, is never, at least until now, fulfilled.

I eat something and then with a little renewed energy I gather up my food sacks and get ready to go. Now having no options but to return to the library, I clamber over blocks of concrete and piles of refuse. Eventually, after looking around carefully I start to see the white rags I had left behind to mark the way back home. It takes me what seems like a long time to make any progress, but who knows the real extent of my present impressions. The sweltering heat and complicated maneuvers slow me down, but I gradually get there.

When I finally arrive, I'm relieved to be back in the library. Thankfully, it is a bit cooler here and I feel somewhat sheltered. I sit down and again take a while to observe my surroundings. What a mess of dust and piles of debris all over the place, but there are the books – the books. I then store the food below my desk and rest for a spell.

For some reason, I randomly start to reflect on explorations and beginnings. I imagine this may have come from previous readings, but I'm not sure. Am I ready for this? Well, I think so, though these topics are both bewildering and complex.

In the midst of my contemplations, poets come to mind. Some have ways with words that configure "possible worlds" and how to view them. Yes, they are creators of powerful images of innovation and impertinence, which careen off the walls of time and sweep over the landscape of life, calling for a re-envision of where it started. And yes, being engaged in the intricate and inquisitive art of exploration is a perpetual challenge, which may come to a provisional end with a refreshing new perception of the beginning. Poetry sometimes deals with such intriguing topics, but I wonder again about exploring 'beginnings.'

After all, the Earth appears to be billions of years old. Not sure what to make of that. Such a vast notion of deep history is mind-blowing, but difficult to avoid.

What was the beginning of the planet and of life on it? How about the eventual and late beginning of humans?

Who knows?

These types of questions had arisen over and over in my life. I had spent hours discussing these and other mysterious matters with family and good friends, notably G, E, and K. We would go this way and then that – back and forth, trying to grapple with the complexity of beginnings. As a respectable primate I always wanted to know, to get it all figured out and tidied up in a satisfactory or even final fashion, but I never managed to get there. The things of beginnings are both too big and too small for a primate to cope with and I soon realized that it was asking the questions, not coming up with all the answers that turned out to be credible and significant. Assumed answers could just no longer bear the weight of the questions, though tentative and carefully thought through conclusions were sometimes a possibility.

Faith again perhaps plays a primordial role. Indeed, beginnings are complicated, yet in spite of that, exploring them is an intriguing and formidable task well worth engaging in.

In the midst of all this, I recall another topic that had beguiled me for years. The subject of endings. Also mysterious and complex. It occurs to me that I might find something in this vast library on both beginnings and endings. While these renowned questions may seem far from daily survival, I somehow can't resist reflecting on them and I hope to discover more of what others thought about such significant issues. I should at some point search through the books to see if I can find something scientific (though I was not a scientist), philosophical, and religious (the latter two were a better fit for me) on these matters. This is something I look forward to doing at an appropriate time, if that ever should present itself.

But I welcome the stories, poems, thoughts, and ideas, which also engage the deep seated notions of beginnings and endings. I wager to myself that they are precious "informers" that spark imagination and shed some light on so much, including my present circumstances, but I also recognize I need to keep searching for other resources 'outside' literature that can possibly give me some clues. Before heading back out of the library I have something to eat and drink. I'm grateful for my supplies and for having the necessary energy, in spite of the heat, to continue to explore potential explanations. I grab an old book, stick it in a bag, and leave.

When I venture back outside I imagine myself getting out of the demolished city and into the countryside in order to see what the situation is like in that environment. I have no idea how far I will have to go or what obstacles might slow me down or even prevent me from doing that. But sometimes when you're willing to imagine something happening ahead of time it actually contributes to it taking place. It's like magic, but not quite. There's no ritual, no spell, no spin of the wheel, just the power of a primate like me imagination envisioning a goal and then realizing it in the material world.

Astonishing!

Remarkable, I suppose, that such a thing even sometimes takes place. There must be some visceral connection between primate imagination and nature. I think it was Einstein who thought along these lines – imagination is the preview of what is to come. Understanding the insights of Einstein may be a highly complex matter, but what is clear is that imagination cannot be excluded from his revolutionary meditations and discoveries, nor should it be from mine.

Wending my way through several streets, using green rags to mark my way back to the library, I notice more and more charred road and space vehicles strewn around in the midst of the rubble. This is indeed a gripping post-apocalyptic scene that I find shocking. No bodies to be found. Not a trace of flesh. It is as if, on the ground and in the sky, the drivers just disappeared. What could have caused this mysterious outcome? Maybe these people were snatched away or destroyed by some high octane force or substance that left no sign of remains. I'm perplexed and troubled, but figure I better move on. What I wager is orange billowy smoke on the horizon means the pollution in the air is still hanging around and will probably never dissipate. Alas, I remember reports of millions of acres being burned, and hundreds of thousands of people evacuated, partially as a result of the climate change ignorance that was peddled about for human and post-human consumption. Such catastrophes became the norm and while there was much debate and discussion about what to do, nothing, primarily due to special interests, was ever done.

I find my way, clambering over concrete blocks and collapsed building wreckage, to the next street. While there are many streets in the city with trees, I think this is the famous street lined with great oaks; marvelous symbols of longevity and strength. These were such magnificent trees, notoriously grand and once a wonder of the ecosystem and a template for the enhancement and enjoyment of nature. Unfortunately, the giants have now been decimated by fire or some other destructive heat force. This saddens me deeply. First the drivers and then the trees gone. It is too much for me to handle. I can't help but be overcome. I sit and weep for some time, how long I can't be sure. After this, even though I'm emotionally spent, my curiosity drives me on, and I decide to continue with what I had first imagined and see if I can make it out of the city to explore the countryside.

Plodding along, climbing from place to place or ducking under the battered remains of buildings, I eventually have to pass through several lengthy caverns to get around obstacles that are totally blocking my way. Inside these passageways, I discover what used to be a number of boutiques. While I'm fearful that what is above me in this tunnel like route will collapse, I'm so intrigued by the shops that I have to stop and look more closely. As I move carefully from one to the other, I notice that the larger artistic creations are severely damaged, but a few smaller exquisite pieces are intact. I choose a silver bracelet, two finely polished emerald tinted stones, and a few gold rings to take back with me to wear and put on my desk. When I turn to leave, part of the wall to my left breaks loose. It misses me by about a meter. I have to quickly step away and cover my mouth and nose because of the cloud of dirt mushrooming up and ready to invade my lungs. My thought - the sooner I get out of this space the better. I leave the shop and re-enter the cavern. I am again struck by the sensation that something or someone is nearby. I head back down the passageway. In the distance I think I see a glowing transparent type figure. It looks grim, pretty horrific, sort of floating or dancing just about where I will need to exit the caverns. Fear rolls over me like pounding waves.

Now what? Could this be a projection from somewhere or is it real?

Who cares, I think to myself. I need to get out of here. In order to avoid this thing I could go back to where I came from, but rubble is falling here and there and the whole edifice might soon cave in. Forced into a spur-of-the-moment decision, I go ahead towards the exit. As I get closer and closer to it, a wall suddenly collapses on my right creating a huge amount of debris and dust, but when I can see again, I notice this has given me a detour that leads me out of the cavern and into the open street. I'm thrilled, in spite of the heat, to be back outside.

Terrified, I press on.

My journey towards the country can now continue. I keep looking behind me, but I don't see any forbidding ghost like thing following me, so for the moment I assume that what I thought I saw was either an illusion, perhaps like so much else that is happening, or whatever it was remained back near the caverns.

Making headway though becomes more and more difficult. Massive blocks of concrete are piled up awfully high, so I have to try to find a place where I can pass through with less effort. Since it dawns on me again that I'm not sure what direction I'm going, I recognize that perhaps I should make up my mind. After contemplating this for some time, how long I'll never know, I decide to go west. So off I go, as best as I can tell, in that direction. Fortunately, I am able to find some less complicated ways to 'climb' over the rubble and at least get somewhere. Since it now becomes easier to make progress, I hope I will be able to eventually arrive at my destination. I'm anxious to get into the shade and to cool off.

It turns out heading west is a good choice. Gradually, I find my way into a space where there are no collapsed buildings or burnt vehicles. This is a wonderful moment and I cherish it. Though, once I finally make it entirely out of the city, I'm brutally disappointed. While the bricks and mortar destruction I left behind is bad enough, the countryside is in a similar state. Most of the trees are scorched, the ground ripped up, and the flowers dead. My hopes of finding something different out here are now ruined. I walk around some, maybe several kilometers, but as far as I can tell it's all the same: devastated. I sit for a while and ponder what this means. Inside myself I shake my head. I'm not really sure.

I then notice it's beginning to get dark.

My first thought is to return to the shelter of the library as quickly as possible. But it is still so hot and soon I won't be able to see much or for that matter detect the green markers that lead me home. Perhaps, I should just stay put for the night and then find my way back when it's lighter. After reflecting on this, my fear of breaking routine and being unsheltered mounts. I think to myself, it is absolutely amazing how I seem to be so easily hooked into routines and motivated by fear.

What should I do?

My decision making process is not improving. Levels of anxiety increase to where my whole body is sort of neuro paralyzed, but I snap out of it, and accept the fact that I need to remain in the countryside and not attempt to return to the library until morning. Even in the best of times some places are just creepier than others, especially when you don't know your environment, and this is one of them. The bizarre shape of the damaged trees and the unusual look of the torn up ground lends itself to imagining all sorts of graphic monster like configurations. Alas, this scary landscape leaves me paranoid and worried about what might lurk in the dark out here, yet this is still the best option in spite of the risk. As dusk is upon me, the last vestiges of light slipping away, I realize I better hurry up and decide where to stay. Arrrgh, another decision.

I survey my possibilities, but have no time to hesitate in the present and growing darkness, so I quickly make up my mind. Seeing a little alcove about ten meters away, I go over to it, and gather for protection some of the smaller tree logs that aren't entirely charcoaled and then flatten a surface of charred grass and loose dirt, so I can lie down when the time comes for sleep. I sit on one of the logs catching the last glimmers of light. For some reason, I find myself revisiting the God question.

Is there some kind of Divine being? Did life come about through a God? Bodily? Soulishly? Consciously? What did Jesus, known as the Christ in New Testament stories, and others, including the scientific informer, have to say about this over the course of time? And why do I even ponder such narratives? I recall hours of fascinating discussions with family and friends about these issues. Surely, the least that can be said is that there is a wide diversity of views on such topics, which have been debated for centuries and even though there's a lot of historical source material, there is simply no way of really knowing, but I can't help asking and no doubt will ask again. Having been lost in my thoughts for some time, how long I'll never know, I feel tremors of exhaustion ripple through my mind and body. It is pretty dark now, so maybe I can sleep. I stretch out on the grass and dirt, try to get comfortable, and must have dozed off. I then wake up to an eerie noise, something like you hear when there's a sonar type sound ringing in your ears and you think you might be entering another dimension. It is still dark. I seem to be in a daze - half awake and half asleep, when I see the gruesome illuminated figure that I had earlier avoided back at the caverns. Chills quickly flow up and down my spine. I'm stunned out of my stupor and now fully awake. I don't dare move and am not sure I can, even if I want to. I wonder if I have actually passed into a new dimension where I'm invisible, and this thing, whatever it is, can't detect my presence, but I'd wager that is not the case. I'm probably after all still a conscious and no doubt visible body of flesh and bones. But the darkness may have come to my aid. The next time I open my eyes, I don't see anything there. I begin to have second thoughts. Perhaps, this 'thing,' as frightening as it looked, is not out to do me any harm. Could it be checking me out and observing my actions to see what I am? Can it hear my thoughts? Detect my emotions?

Who knows?

I never get back to sleep. Gradually, the darkness fades, and I want to change my mood, so I get up and cautiously go over and pick up the book I had brought from the library. Such a beautiful volume. I gather it was produced with great creativity and skill. Fortunately, it has not been damaged. It turns out to be an anthology of ancient texts, so the content is also a marvel. There are law codes, treaties, contracts, myths, letters, hymns, and epics. In the pre-dawn light I read one. Just then the sun appears through the thick clouds. For a fleeting moment it looks like an amazing ball of fire lighting up the world. The colors are vivid and sublime. It's no wonder, I thought, that some ancients worshipped the sun and at least one even wrote a hymn to it. Akhenaton, King of Egypt, apparently composed the lines I have just been reading:

Thou appearest beautifully on the horizon of heaven,
Thou living Aton, the beginning of life!
When thou art risen on the eastern horizon,
Thou hast filled every land with thy beauty.
Thou art gracious, great, glistening, and high over every land;
Thy rays encompass the lands to the limit of all that thou hast made:
As thou art Re, thou reachest to the end of them;
(Thou) subduest them (for) thy beloved son.

Though thou art far away, thy rays are on earth;
Though thou art in their faces, no one knows thy going.

I can't get over how stunning this hymn is. Simply marvelous. It was grappling with 'meaning making' concerning something that seemed to be transcendent. In doing so, the author was expressing a belief in a monotheistic source for all of life, contrary to the polytheistic views of his time. His imaginative and significant musings attempted to locate and explain a piece of the puzzle of the world in a new way.

I find that intriguing!

This book is so interesting I could keep reading for hours, but I need to try to return to the library. After discovering that the countryside is a disaster, I don't have regrets about leaving. There isn't much here that will help me understand what is going on, nor give me any relief from the pressures of absence and loss. I'm determined to keep on searching.

I'm glad to find the last green marker I had left behind to show me the way. The trek back to the library is going to be difficult and I am not looking forward to climbing over the boulders and struggling through the wreckage and debris again. I surely don't want to stay somewhere else when it's dark, so I just have to get there. I start out. It's a little easier at the outset, so that's encouraging. When I have forged on for a while, I'll never know how long, I come across some intriguing architectural constructs. Due to my freaked out state after my frightening encounter with the 'white' thing, I hadn't noticed them on my way out. In spite of the damaged state of these works, I can still see they are mind blowing creative acts from the past. An attempt to immortalize a way of life; a way of saying, doing, and being that someone thought important enough to be sculpted into time, space, and memory. Phenomenal, even though they're just barely recognizable.

It's as if someone or something wanted to wipe out traces of human primate splendor and creativity, yet was not entirely successful. Surely, there must be some reason for all this, but whatever it is, it continues to elude me. As I move on from one mountain of rubble to another I'm again struck by the devastated character of the landscape, though at the same time utterly shocked by little gems of leftover beauty. When I slow my harried, even at times frantic pace, I turn to my left and see an exquisite arched portal leading to a partially standing building. I'm intrigued by this imagery and ponder it, how long I'll never know, then take a detour to explore what's inside. Once I get through the gateway and into the remains of the structure, I discover hundreds of maps, pictures of space configurations; planets, galaxies, and the uni-multiverse. I figure this must have been a physics and astronomy institute or sort of think tank place. How some of this survived the heat, cold, water, and avalanche of destruction is beyond me.

What a gold mine!

I'm neither a physicist nor an astronomer, but some of this data confirms what is already somewhat clear to me. The measurable uni or multiverse is big. Well, actually it's immensely huge. Vast. Seemingly unending. So much space and more space. And that's just what is thought to be measureable. It is also estimated that there are trillions of stars and galaxies. This is amazing and totally mind boggling, even to try to imagine. In addition, the Earth is billions of years old. Primates like me actually lived in a sliver of a sliver of reality and for a relatively short period of time; though many of them came to believe that planet Earth and their species were at the center of everything. Nothing is further from what these documents claim is really the case. I could have spent days here and might at some point later, but I need to get back to the library before dark. I leave several yellow markers behind to help me find the location again. So on I go, out through the archway.

Making my way through the debris is as arduous as ever. Lots of work. I can't stop reflecting on the momentous size of the uni or multiverse as I plod on. Why is it so big? Maybe it was waiting for something remarkable to happen, though this remains only one possibility among others. I really have no idea. Up ahead of me I can see the caverns. I immediately get paranoid and look for a way to avoid these, fearing an altercation with the dreadful figure that had previously appeared to me both here and in the country. But this still seems my best option to make it to the other side of the impassible obstacles. And perhaps this 'white' thing means me no harm or isn't even there. After some time of contemplating, not sure how long, I decide to just go for it and get through as quickly as I can. No stopping to admire what is down here this time. In my rush to get to the other end, I don't pay attention to what is on the ground. Half way there, I trip over a cable and after almost catching myself, go down. It feels like I tear up my knee and maybe sprain an ankle on the same leg. At first I try not to move, as the sensations after a fall can turn out to be either better or worse than first assumed. Fear ripples through me, but I gingerly sit up to assess the damage. My knee is bleeding. I'm able to bend and flex it, so I guess that maybe there is merely a deep gash under the blood. I roll up my pants to have a better look and find oozing blood running down my calf. Grabbing onto the wall, I pull myself up and gently put weight on my leg. When I attempt to walk, the ankle seems a little weak, but not sprained. So, it isn't as serious as I initially thought. I need to stop the bleeding of my knee and if that works I can perhaps make it back to the library before dark. I pull out one of my green markers and clean off the blood. I then tie one of them around my knee and the bleeding seems to slow and I hope it will eventually stop. After this, I hobble the rest of the way through the caverns and out into the street. Once there, I look out to my right and see a tantalizingly bright orange stairway leading up into the sky. I can't make out where the top is, so I have no idea how far it goes. I ponder the pros and cons of seeing where this stairway may take me. Who knows what I might find along the way or at the top? Maybe there'll be some answers to my questions. But my leg is a bother. I consider, for how long I'll never know, and finally start up. Soon I get into mist. I can't see very well, and then all of a sudden, out of the murky sky there are several ghoulish like creatures that appear. They don't come near me, but beckon me on to keep climbing. Fear gets the best of me and I wager this isn't a favorable environment for finding out much about why I am here alone and what is happening to me. I turn and edge back down the stairway to the street. My knee starts to bleed some again, but the ankle is fine. When I get back down the weather has changed. It is freezing. Figuring I better head straight back to the library and not take any further detours, I slowly make my way along and arrive before dark.

It is a huge relief to be back in the familiar surroundings of the library. I eat and drink and care for my knee and then take a short rest. Since there is just enough light to read something, I pick up another book of poetry. There is nothing like a poem to ramp up imagination. I'm ready. I'm looking forward to engaging with the splendid thoughts, words, and images that might be inscribed across the screen of time, which has, in one form at least, all but disappeared for me. This poem is written by W. B. Yeats, 1920, and is titled:

'The Second Coming'

Turning and turning in the widening gyre
The falcon cannot hear the falconer;
Things fall apart; the centre cannot hold;
Mere anarchy is loosed upon the world,
The blood-dimmed tide is loosed, and everywhere
The ceremony of innocence is drowned;
The best lack all conviction, while the worst
Are full of passionate intensity.

Surely some revelation is at hand;
Surely the Second Coming is at hand.
The Second Coming! Hardly are those words out
When a vast image out of *Spiritus Mundi*
Troubles my sight: somewhere in sands of the desert
A shape with lion body and the head of a man,
A gaze blank and pitiless as the sun,
Is moving its slow thighs, while all about it
Reel shadows of the indignant desert birds.
The darkness drops again; but now I know
That twenty centuries of stony sleep
Were vexed to nightmare by a rocking cradle,
And what rough beast, its hour come round at last,
Slouches towards Bethlehem to be born?

Such relentless provocative words are remarkably pertinent to life and
death among other things. I deeply connect with this poem and Yeats
definitely has a striking way of describing something that resonates with

some of my own feelings and thoughts about my present circumstances in the world.

Wow, just wow!

My imagination is soaring. Read these words again:

"Things fall apart; the centre cannot hold;
Mere anarchy is loosed upon the world.
The blood-dimmed tide is loosed, and everywhere
The ceremony of innocence is drowned;"

These lines are so poignantly crafted; it is as if they could be written for my own day. Crushingly sublime, horrifically true, especially now. And the rest. Well, I can use some revelation and the Second Coming. I wonder about that. So many images and metaphors.

Marvelous reflections.

As the last slivers of light disappear, I'm ready for sleep. I'm so tired and it's still freezing, so I retrieve my cardboard bedding and wrap myself up in hopes of staying warm enough through the night. These extreme and fast paced weather changes are destructively deconstructing my biological rhythms and cadences. The stunning poem by Yeats is churning and turning in my mind and through my imagination. Such evocative pictures in words keep me at first from sleeping, as I long to understand more and more of this Yeats poem, but eventually I doze off.

When I awake, I lie there in my cardboard covering for a spell. I'm surprisingly pretty warm. I drift off and then vividly remember a stunning dream I had. I was taken by a seer or prophet of some sort to the underworld. Inside this gloomy gray dark chasm there were breathing shapes referred to as shades – the dead, or so I was told. Apparently, this place of the dead was a legend in ancient Greek thought.

But what dead? Humans.

Whether these previous humans were passing through or here forever, I didn't have a clue. The shades seemed to move around in silhouette form, but never got very far. Baffling. I wondered and then asked the seer/prophet. Why are they here? Are they searching for flesh? To be re-embodied? No response. After all I thought to myself, even though human bodies are fragile and wear out, it appears they're all that humans have to be represented in the material world. Were disembodied, but somehow surviving humans, being kept cordoned off from any contact with physicality? If this place was any indication to go by, once the body was gone it didn't seem possible to recover it, but according to the seer/prophet there could be exceptions to that in the future for all one knew. This brought to light the age old, long debated, and complex matter of the afterlife; indeed such a perplexing topic. Humans had pondered their fate after death over and over for centuries. Everyone appeared to die, but then what happens, I asked the seer? Response: For some, two prominent options arise: heaven or hell, but for the most part these are opaque and controversial possibilities. For others, it is assumed that there is a full stop at death – existence is simply terminated. Nobody survives the loss of breath as human life. For still others, there is a body and a spirit or soul. At death the body decomposes, but the soul or spirit lives on in perhaps some intermediate state. At this point, my dream came to an end, and of course, unfortunately without any resolution or at least dream-like answers. Perhaps, this issue of the afterlife is one of the best examples of the conflict of interpretations that primates like me have wrestled with throughout their history. From the emergence of their beginnings, it seems, humans had and continue to have a foreboding fear of death, as myths, plays, and epitaphs demonstrate. Thousands of texts have been written, millions of questions asked. I can't help and reflect and wonder about what all this controversy means. But then I think why I am where I am is a big enough mystery for me, without trying to figure out if people were going to survive in the afterlife or going anywhere or not after death, but the question is nevertheless poignantly inevitable and thus worthwhile considering, and I guess even more so in my circumstances. What will be my outcome; my future, my destiny?

I need to get up now and change my thoughts. I start with some warming up exercise to get things going. I intensely concentrate on trying to stay physically and mentally fit, but it's difficult. It is important not to let either of these dimensions go, even though I'm not exactly sure why. After working out, so to speak, I then eat and drink something, before reading another story.

This narrative is centered on the deep and dreadful tragedy of war. It was a story of no longer being able to choose your values and goals, of being prisoners in thought and speech, but how in spite of this, some people were able to covertly subvert the corrupt and power hungry despots who sought to control the world and its people through brain numbing propaganda and military force. The principle characters in the book were members of the Muller family; Louisa, 45, clever, daring, and action oriented; Henry, 47, reflective, patient, and cautious, and their two capable and intelligent children Jacob and Jutta, both in their twenties. Henry was an engineer and expert carpenter, Louisa a soil consultant and savvy electrician, and Jutta and Jacob studied architecture. They made up a small, but super-efficient band of resistance that helped thousands to escape the grip of death, even though they could have easily profited financially by joining forces with the powerful war machine. Here's how they did it: Dedication, efficiency, and hard work, among other things, including digging two tunnels. These tunnels were about a thousand meters long and it took careful planning and considerable effort to build them. The Muller family unit had the abilities and they worked together as a team in a complementary and competent way. Loyalty, honor, and morality marked their lives, in a world of betrayal and injustice. They put themselves in serious peril to rescue others. The family lived in a neutral, but not to be trusted country, close to the borders of two other countries at war. The first tunnel went from their country to the north and into enemy territory. It was extremely difficult to get the persecuted out, yet there were friends in the north who were willing to risk their lives for others and arrange an escape via the tunnels. The second tunnel went from their country to the west, also enemy held territory, but with a strong covert resistance that was particularly efficient in meeting people when they came out and then taking them into hiding. Night travel to the tunnels was safest, but not without danger. This story recounted several spine tingling near catastrophes and many courageous escapes. One evening, for example, there were about three hundred women, men, and children hiding in the thick bushy forest ready to enter the two tunnels. They had traveled a long ways and it was imperative that they get through, since there was no turning back now. The resistance was waiting for them in the west and everything was prepared. Though rare in this region, a night border patrol just happened to pass that evening. Thousands had previously escaped through the tunnels, but perhaps this time they all, including the Muller family, would be caught and executed. As the patrol was passing nearby, a man panicked and turned to run. He tripped over a dangling tree branch and thought he broke his leg. He started to howl in pain, which should have alerted the patrol, but with the noise on the road of the jeep rak-traks, fortunately the patrol didn't hear anything. Someone quickly quieted him and looked at his leg, which in the end was badly bruised, but not broken. He would be able to walk with help. At this point, they had to now wait for the patrol to return and pass by in the other direction, before making a move towards the tunnels. This seemed to take hours and some thought they should risk crossing the road, since dawn was fast approaching. But they waited. Soon after this, the patrol indeed passed on its return and they finally were able to go for it. Hundreds of people, under the Muller family's supervision, flooded out of the forest, across the road, into the first tunnel, and then the second, and out into the waiting arms of the resistance. This escape was a grand success and much celebrated, as many others had been previously. Unfortunately, in the days to come the patrols increased. It was as if the enemy knew what had been going on, and was just waiting for another attempt, when it would slaughter all those waiting to escape. This never happened, since at that point the Muller family fled their country by going through their own tunnel and crossing the western border. They continued fighting with the resistance, only now in other ways. Their contribution to the quest for freedom remained outstanding and committed. Eventually, when the enemy was defeated and the war over, their tremendous work was acknowledged by governments and people from all over the world who expressed their deepest gratitude.

I learn much from this tragic, yet rich, and rewarding story. A couple of things stand out.

War killed millions.

Nothing in the whole of the world was so pitifully awful. There were thousands left dead on site and hundreds of thousands buried in cemeteries across the world. The industry, brutality, and horror of war partially showed what primates like me evolved into, but the valor of the Muller family, the friends, and other members of the resistance displayed the other side of that evolution: sacrifice, empathy, and care. This representation of such a conflicted picture of humanity in the narrative is indeed an enigma and it lures me into further reflections. Why do primates like me have diametrically opposed interests, goals, and motivations? Racism, hate, and injustice proliferate in the human niche and are awful, yet in spite of this, equality, love, and justice refuse to surrender. I'd wager that there are different kinds of wars, including wars of ideas, not fought with laser weapons and ballistic bombs, but with words, thoughts, and actions. So, in this story 'war' runs along several lines and has a multiplicity of meanings, but as good as this narrative is it still leaves me without resolution to the age old question of why war took place or why I am here alone. But, of course, I think to myself, no story can answer that, can it? Maybe the human race had wiped itself out over a relatively short period of time, not due to a major war, but built as it were off the formidable increase of across the board neglect in every area of the environment, resulting in a multifarious and instantaneous collapse and ecological planetary devastation.

Who knows?

I leave the library again in search of new "informers" that will hopefully explain and help me understand my circumstances. The enigma of beginnings and endings continues to weigh heavily on me. When I get outside, it's sweltering. I tie a rag on my head. In order to make headway through the piles of rubble, I have to concentrate on each step. If I'm not careful, I could break a leg or twist an ankle or even fall into a hole. These are ever present dangers that plague me and tire me out.

After creeping along over numerous obstacles, sometimes on all fours, I turn into what looks like it used to be an alleyway. I have not been here before, so this is unknown territory. It appears to be one way in and one out – a dead end. Moving slowly further in, I notice a gathering of some sort a short distance off. Initially, I think, perhaps I'm not alone after all. This sends shots of adrenaline through my system. In my excitement to engage, I remain calm and think I should be vigilant. I stop and ponder and ask myself some questions. Is this dangerous? How close can I get? Should I attempt to make contact? Are they perhaps reliable "informers" of the fate of the Earth and of my situation? Edging on cautiously, I get to a place where I can see, but I hope not be seen. From this vantage point I notice that the figures in the group are wearing black hooded robes and creative carnival like masks. They are kind of leaning over in a circle, without making a sound. I can't tell if these are humans, techno-sapiens, robots or what.

Should I get closer?

The atmosphere is weird and the whole thing strikes me as some kind of séance or ritual, so I keep my distance. A blue fluorescent gleaming light all of a sudden appears above the group and seems to attract its attention. Brilliant rays flow out of the source towards each member in an electrifying sort of way that connects them all together. This powerful energy streaming must give force to these nebulous beings, as they now appear as translucent and focused.

But for what?

I then hear a buzzzzzing like sound, which seems to come from the blue gleaming light and goes on for some time; how long I'll never know. This could perhaps be a form of communication within the group, yet I'm not at all sure that is the case. When the sound eventually fades away, the hooded figures bow to the light, and instantly disintegrate. They literally disappear and the blue light streaks off into the sky at hyper speed. Perplexed, I sit and try to make sense of what I think just happened. I'm actually not really sure what happened, if anything at all. There is nothing tangible like the bricks and mortar strewn around to convince me that what I think I saw and heard is actually believable. But surely, I reflect again, not only the 'seen' is worth believing and even it can sometimes be deceptive. There may be all kinds of "possible worlds" that merit belief, including the 'unseen.' I even wonder if I have cosmic opponents or advocates who are fighting it out. Might there be an invisible battle behind the scenes that determines what happens in the visible world? Probably superstition, but there is so much I don't know. After some time, I have no idea how long, I leave the alleyway and go back out to the debris filled street.

I carry on and venturing into new territory, I make sure I mark my way with gray tattered rags. From what I can tell, this part of the city must be an industrial zone. Rummaging through the remains of several enterprises I eventually enter what probably used to be a massive hangar type building with a charred Mars XXX sign hanging off it and a host of battered national flags strewn around on the ground. I have no idea why or how many nations are represented. I see plenty of shattered video surveillance cameras, which indicates to me that this must have been a high security site. It is hard work trudging on into this collapsed shell. There are piles of steel and other shiny metal pieces lying around and this makes it slippery and difficult to get footing. I manage, but have to be careful. I then come across numerous signs of precision crafted machine parts and what looks like an assembly line. There are rows and rows of smashed computers and huge robotic manufacturing arms on both sides of the line. Everything is covered with heaps of dust and debris, but I notice far to the left and standing out from the rubble, an enormous blue vehicle/ transporter. After looking it over a bit, I wonder how many could get on this state of the art creation. I estimate maybe three thousand, maybe five thousand, maybe more? Then I think, perhaps a large scale project had developed in many of the industrialized nations of the world (which would explain the flags), to get humans and others off the Earth. For decades humans had talked about leaving Earth and going to another planet that could potentially sustain them or at least some of them. The climate scene was a disaster. Severe lightning storms caused raging fires burning millions of homes and acres of forests. Combined with this torrid heat, massive rainfalls brought devastating floods destroying life and property on a global scale. As the environment and atmosphere degenerated and were on the verge of destruction, these vehicles may have served as space shuttles used for evacuating humans, techno-sapiens, and robots, and there might possibly be thousands of them in various locations around the world.

What a thought! What a prospect! Could those beings who still survived on Earth have made a mass exit to another planet? From what I see in this hangar, even in the midst of its present state, the ingenuity and technology had been available.

Who knows?

After sitting down and imagining different scenarios, I come to the conclusion that this "informer" has given me some interesting clues. I will continue to reflect on them, but now need to move on before dark to explore other locations. Just as I had complications getting into this huge structure, it is equally difficult to get out and back to the street. There is no clear pathway to take. I keep moving, but don't seem to make much progress. I look up and notice razor sharp sheets of gray and black steel dangling menacingly from what used to be the roof and fear an avalanche from above that could cut my flesh in two. Proceeding gingerly, for how long I'll never know, I gradually find my way through the mess of metal shards and emerge from the building without injury.

Rambling up the same demolished street, I pass several other smaller manufacturing sites that may have been connected to the massive one I just left. They all have Mars XXX signs hanging off them in one form or another, so this scenario seems likely. Quite an operation! But I do wonder if anybody or anything actually got on one of these vehicles. Probably. Veering off to the west for what must have been a few kilometers, I enter into a different part of the city, but will probably return to the Mars XXX site later at some point.

A quick observation of some of the partially standing structures gives me the impression that this was a corporate financial and business center. There are what looks like corporate office buildings, banks, and insurance companies. So much I think, for investments, wealth, and being insured in case of disaster and devastation.

None of that matters now.

Perhaps, from what I can tell, the chaos unleashed by humanity and its abuse of the natural world came to mean that all that mattered was survival and whether you were rich or poor became entirely irrelevant in this sort of world. Alas, no time for digging around in this area right now, as I need to make my way back to the library. This is always an arduous task and I don't expect anything different this time.

Following my gray markers is helpful, but having to cross over piles of unstable wreckage make walking as complicated as ever. I look at my shoes and realize that I better get something more adequate soon. Maybe I can find a pair that would be protective, something like work shoes with a steel toe or a reinforced pair of hiking boots. Almost anything would be better than the black & white sneakers I'm wearing. Considering the terrain and my worn out shoes, I make decent progress until I suddenly encounter a dazzlingly colorful clown like character. I can't be sure if this is a projection of some kind, an AI program, or a 'real' clown. The reputation of clowns was always pretty ambiguous and unsettled. They were often portrayed as charming and humorous, but also as dastardly and violent, unleashing havoc and discontent. It seemed to me that clowns tended to be luminous sorts of in-between figures; mythological, mystical, or even post-human. At any rate, this clown, in some ways similar to a Marcel Marceau, the veritable master of the art from the past, gives me a threateningly hilarious performance that is out of this world; utterly brilliant and captivating.

Bravo!

I'm fascinated and completely taken in by the unpredictable clowning, which generates a "possible world" that I can enter and inhabit, at least for a spell. I then notice that the clown, before it disintegrates, as many of the previous appearances of phenomena had tended to do, gestures in the direction of what may have been an old theater. The edifice is almost entirely collapsed. Not sure if I should trust the clown, considering some of my previous experiences. So, I am a bit hesitant to go over and explore further, but finally after some time of reflecting on the genius of the clown's performance, how long I'll never know, I go and check it out. Impressive! This must have once been a very special place. There are some seats in view and the walls and decorative remains speak of a remarkable venue for a clown troupe and its audience. In the midst of the wreckage, I find a damaged billboard with a poster on it. After dusting it off some, I am able to make out what it says. This was an ad or announcement for a clown presentation entitled: *The End of the World.*

Wow! Interesting!

Clowns had the ability to mock society and were often cleverly critical of injustice and corruption. So, here was another hint that things were getting worse before the final deterioration and decay of the planet Earth. The insight of clowns was precious in this environment, but it still doesn't give me an explanation or understanding of the events that left me alone in the world. Before exiting the ruins of the theater, something exquisitely colorful catches my eye. Moving in that direction, I perceive what looks like hundreds of clown costumes, but the weird thing about this is that these costumes have the appearance of being 'real' clowns. It is like the clown outfits contained something or someone, but there are no bodies, no faces, and no clowns. Disappeared? As I leave, I wonder what happened here.

Who knows?

Reflecting on the encounter with the clown(s) makes me sort of sad, but also appreciative of all the good clowns had given to the world. I suppose this may be the way some of them saw themselves. Clowns had a unique talent to move your emotions from sorrow to joy and to touch everything in-between. Splendid! Their creative genius was often extraordinarily affirmative, though sometimes mischievous and disturbing. I think to myself that maybe I should look for a book about the history of clowning, or what it's like to be a clown, written by a clown. That would be intriguing.

As I continue on my way back to the library, I look carefully for some place that had sold shoes. I don't see anything for the moment, so I just carry on. Fortunately or unfortunately, as the case may be, this time there are no further detours or encounters. When I finally reach the library, I'm drained. It is a pleasure to be back in what has become something of a haven and to be able to eat and drink. I settle in and just rest some. Later, I go through the rubble and pick up more books to put next to my desk. Sorting through these new volumes, I notice another book of poetry. I open it and read some lines of a poem by Emily Dickinson, written around 1862.

I reason, Earth is short –
And Anguish – absolute –
And many hurt,
But, what of that?

I reason, we could die –
The best Vitality
Cannot excel Decay,
But, what of that?

I reason, that in Heaven –
Somehow, it will be even –
Some new Equation, given –
But, what of that?

What a jewel! This sublime poem is marvelous. I read it several times. I'm drawn to both its simplicity and profundity. My imagination spikes and I'm transported into the "possible world" of the poem that somehow through words is so deeply connected to my own. The Earth, Anguish, hurt, the insufficiency of Vitality in the face of Decay, and the hope that in Heaven it would be *even*; that there might be a new way of figuring out matters. In some sense though, this seems to remain open, not to be made too much of in the present circumstances. The power of words is remarkable. I then wonder how poetry had fared in a supposedly post-truth world.

This reminds me of several serious discussions with friends and family over the years concerning whether or not *truth* was knowable. While living in an age of conflict, complexity, and change, these controversial debates had come to be at the root of the human primate niche and formed, as it were, something of the back story of a variety of mediatized front story scenarios, often uncritically consumed by the public at large. The question of truth and then post-truth was massive and touched almost every area of life, including history, politics, economics, philosophy, science, and religion.

Those who were for being able to know the truth argued that all is self-evident, objective, and absolute. Everything is crystal clear. Only facts, no interpretations. Those who were against being able to know the truth claimed that all is self-authenticated, subjective, and relative. Everything is blurry. No facts, only interpretations. This world had become more and more polarized and mediators were few and far between.

I'd wager, admitting that there isn't total truth does not necessarily lead to total relativism. Neither extremes are plausible options. What's true and what's relative would seem to have to be considered by degrees, not totalities, since those were just not available. Something like in-between truths for in-between times is more or less applicable to life as I see it. Sufficient degrees of truthfulness can sometimes be fitting across the board, without making them absolute truths; while at other times, they'll be pertinent only for a particular context and circumstance that has to be part of a much bigger picture. Alas, I'm not sure how much of this matters to my life now, but somehow I still want to know more truth than I presently have, not that I can ever have it all. Surely, the forces of being a primate like me and thus curious and wanting to resolve, though limited and finite, are strongly in play. Ouch! Blessing or curse?

Then, I have another thought. Poets were often well known protesters. Protest, I'd wager, is a negation of relativism, even if protesters don't always realize this. They may hold a range of views on some issues, but when it comes to what they're protesting for or against there's only one view that's true. Truth rocks, at least in the context of protest. But like the famed encounter between Jesus of Nazareth and Pilate, as recounted in a story in the biblical text, the inescapable and massive question that Pilate poses to Jesus remains valid: what is truth? During this meeting between Pilate and Jesus no answer was given. As a result, storytellers, poets, and the rest of humanity have been searching for it for centuries.

After reflecting further on these "truth" discussions and enigmas, I'm as perplexed as ever. But maybe that is as it should be. Primate brains like mine tend to want to do away with uncertainty and put it all together and that may be a huge mistake, if mystery is the better option.

At any rate, I think I need a change of ideas and to read something different before going to sleep. I pick up one of the books I had brought back to my desk earlier and start reading. This story is about Sophia, a young woman who was struggling with identity and selfhood. My interest is sparked and I keep reading and reading – I think to myself, I wrestle with this too. Who doesn't?

Sophia was intelligent, sensitive, and intense, but because of low self-worth, these healthy character traits, for her, did not amount to much. Her view of herself, was largely due to her family background, which was unhealthy and caused a fair amount of turmoil in her life. Guilt trips, subtle and blatant forms of verbal abuse, manipulation, and undermining of self-confidence were several of the many unfortunate consequences Sophia experienced growing up as an only child with wildly dysfunctional perfectionist parents. This led her into several difficulties including, confusion, destructive tendencies, fear of failing to measure up, and self-hate. In spite of years of living in this awful environment, she excelled in school and was awarded a scholarship to attend a major university, studying psychology, philosophy, and literature. This funding allowed her to get away from her parents and the freedom to start thinking for herself.

She realized that competing voices floated around in her head like butterflies on a spring day. Deciding which ones to listen to was her ongoing challenge. But to sort this out she needed help from someone she could trust. There were several counselors at the university and Sophia decided to meet up with one. After several consultations and spending many hours together in discussion, a relationship of trust was built. Sophia gradually recognized that she had good support and that her counselor herself had struggled with similar issues. As the story unfolds, the counselor's observations and insights, and Sophia's reflections, went something like this.

The bold and cutting voice of inappropriate accusation, condemnation, and guilt that results in self-hate is often so loud that it prevents Sophia from hearing the voice of appropriate freedom, capacity, and encouragement, which results in self-love. Changing what she listens to, therefore, is essential to living a well-lived life. This change cannot happen through an act of the will alone, although the will may challenge her to listen again. Sophia learned more about this over time. In personal struggles with self-hate an appeal to an Act of the will is essential to combat such falsehoods, but it can never be an end in and of itself. She discovered, as her counselor suggested, that trying to "will" self-hate to diminish was not a sustainable enterprise. That is, the will has to find its bearings in a larger context, which includes multiple "informers" capable of offering a reorientation towards an appropriate and viable self-love. What Sophia was in desperate need of is a line of appeal that goes beyond the will and which acknowledges that there is to some extent more objective criteria available that potentially heightens the volume of the voice that is a precious resource for self-love. A seemingly insurmountable antagonism towards self – self-hate – read as a continual experience of fault, guilt, and denial, undid Sophia and the lack of dialogue robbed her of a deep part of who she was. An embrace of a dialogue with other reliable "informers" could help to validate appropriate trust and suspicion, and thereby expose self-hate as a lie, eventually replacing it with a finite, yet genuine picture of a truer self to love and be loved, in the configuration of oneself as another. Sophia though finds going against misplaced trust is a struggle. She is so convinced by the standards that she set for herself or that have been imposed upon her, that she never considers that she might need to be suspicious of them. Her counselor pointed out that standards of measure have to be discovered, questioned, and assessed. Contraband all too easily finds its way into our lives and as it does, we can often end up embracing a false standard. Sophia's embrace of illegitimate guilt and bogus condemnation were unfaithful resources that kept her bound to the dubious legalities of measuring up to what's deceptive. Slowly, with the help of her counselor and through many ups and downs along the way, Sophia started to become aware of inappropriate trust and attuned to credible suspicion along these lines, and as she did she could take action against the false standards. This wasn't easy, since it included a reversal of identity and a letting go of the counterfeit, which had influenced and shaped her for far too long. Sophia found that systems of compensation for failed standard keeping never work. They are corrosive and rust the insides. A hope of achieving an "OK" self if she "overdid that" and therefore "does this" will fail. True, there may be a place for standards in life, but they can't be the grounding of who she perceived herself to be. The problem is that the "overdid that" and "do this" won't give her what she longed for – an ability to accept herself because of who she is and in spite of who she is not. Sophia learned for herself that value, dignity, and worth are "already there" and thus not something that she earns by measuring or failing to measure up to self-made standards. Undoing the false pictures and perspectives that her parents had imposed on her and that to some degree she had embraced, set her free to move in new directions. While the unending work of the interpretation of her actions remained, Sophia was in a much better place to be able to discern, evaluate, and understand a truer picture of her selfhood and identity than ever before. She went on to graduate from university with honors and later became a counselor helping people like herself, which she found to be a great comfort.

This was a marvelous story and interesting to read. I think there are several takeaways from this impressive little book. I really admire Sophia and her courage to wrestle with her issues and to seek out counsel.

Figuring out something more of who she was, turned out to be a massive and complex question. She was unwilling to give in to her parents' portrayal of her and chose to work with her trust and suspicion perspectives developing insights to connect and re-connect them in different and healthier ways than she had previously done. I greatly appreciated her counselor, who was devoted and took the time and energy to interact with her in meaningful ways, which ended up making a huge difference in her life.

Reflecting a bit further, it seems to me that selfhood and identity are a given and also have to be fought for because life is this fascinating dialogue between what has been, what already is, and what is yet to come.

Wow!

Now it is getting dark, and that means it's time for sleep. Since the polar cold is back, I find my cardboard bed covering and wrap myself up in hopes of staying warm enough through the night.

The next morning, I awake to a fierce glacial wind. It seems colder to the bone than it probably is, but nonetheless I'm freezing. This cold northerly gusting, la bise, as it is called in some parts of the world, makes it very uncomfortable and leaves me feeling even less settled. In spite of being jittery, I get up and do my workout hoping that deep breaths help some and that this crazy wind will soon subside so I can get warmer.

Now before anything else, let me just say that all that has happened so far is quite mesmerizing ....

What's it all about anyway?

After eating and drinking something, I leave the library in search of my destiny and perhaps a clearer understanding and explanation for my present state. The wind dies down and it actually is a bit warmer, though still cold. I take some purple rags with me as markers since I'm heading in a new direction, which takes me through several "post-streets" and a decimated open plaza type square where beings probably met up and socialized. I then venture into what seems to be a now dilapidated high tech hospital or clinic. Screens are strewn about and the remains give some kind of picture of what medicine had become. Beds arranged close together with cables attached to them in what looks like massive ward structures, hundreds of block long corridors with intact digital monsters, pharma drug packaging lying on the ground. I recall that machines had long been responsible for human health and AI played a key role in deciding whether a life was worth the expense and energy it would take to prolong it. Human value and relational contexts started to be entirely ignored when it came to life and death. Many humans were appalled at such treatment and decision making, but to no avail. There was no way to resist the imposition of power, where the bottom line was always what was cost effective. This brutal policy meant that thousands who could have lived longer healthy lives didn't. They were abruptly terminated and forgotten just because of some notion of programmed efficiency in what was alluded to as the age of progress. In these days, institutions, whether medical, political, or otherwise, dominated the landscape of human existence and bureaucratic tech reigned over the decision making process for all concerned.

I'm stunned by what I see next. There are what appear to be human like bones in the clutter, but as I go further I find half skeletons and then whole ones. No question. These primates were humans. Turns out they are scattered all over the place, long having become part of the debris.

How long? Not a clue.

I wonder what happened to these beings. Was there some kind of huge disconnection where the machines simply stopped functioning: no electricity, failed generators, and thus everyone in the place died and was left without burial or cremation?

Whatever happened to 'care'?

There is some evidence here that those who had serious medical issues were left to die. What I can't discern however, is if this was an accident or done on purpose, or if there was some other explanation.

Who knows?

At any rate, I regret having entered this horrific site, so with no answers to my questions and with a sense of profound sorrow, I leave as quickly as possible. Stumbling around now away from the skeletons is a relief, but I still can't help re-imagining over and over what I have just seen and what caused it. You probably know how it is when something is like branded into imagination and continually replays itself. I sit down to reflect, while the awful visuals of bones and skeletons, along with my thoughts and questions reverberate around inside my space. I ask myself again what happened and mourn the fact that humans seemed to have lost freedom, a place for personal integrity, and the principle of trust, to a power where machines controlled important and intimate decisions concerning the future of the vulnerable and those in ill-health. The dominating power might have first stolen the moral high ground in the name of security and proficiency, but this probably quickly led to oppression and loss of choice, since the machines always knew best. Not sure how long I ponder all this, and I guess I'll never know, but the gravity of it weighs heavily on me for some time. I try to put it together with my previous explorations, especially in the industrial section. I imagine that all healthy primates like me boarded or were forced to board space shuttles headed to another planet. They might have abandoned an unsustainable Earth with its climate calamities, terrible wars, and vicious plagues, largely attributable to human irresponsibility, for a supposedly safer environment. On the other hand, maybe there were massive death zones on the Earth where humans destroyed each other, or were consumed by some lethal force spewed across the planet. Not sure? Nothing's undisputable.

Eventually, I get up and head across the piles of rubble to see what I might find. I'm more determined than ever to keep looking for clues about what happened. When I turn around, I'm struck by something I had not previously perceived: an oval shaped opening that looks like it goes into the underground. It is as if it has appeared out of nowhere. I'm sort of tempted to enter, but think this is probably pretty crazy. Everything might cave in.

What do I expect to learn here?

I go back and forth about this, but my curiosity gets the better of me this time, so eventually I go in. I start off and move through a kind of labyrinth – a tunnel like maze of different directions. At first it is fine, but after I go a fair way in, it gets darker and darker and now I'm not sure where I am or which way is out. This spooks me some. I start to use my hands to feel along the walls as I go further in. From time to time patches of light appear, but they are ephemeral. As I turn left and then right several times I suddenly think I hear voices. I stop, yet I can't make anything out - nothing is clear since the sound is something like a low mumble. I begin to wonder if there are others in here. Maybe someone was left behind or had chosen to hide in the labyrinth? Fear and anticipation flow through my brain and body. Who might this be? A primate like me? Another language user? This buildup of expectation continues as I keep moving. I swerve around another brick in the wall and turn rightish, but creep along slowly because it is now really dark. Gradually my excitement wanes since as I go on, I hear only silence - nothing. I think to myself, one of the great defeater's of hope is silence. Disappointed and still not having any idea of where I'm going, I don't know how or where to turn back, so I have no choice other than to press on deeper into the labyrinth. I hope, though I'm now getting more panicky, I'll discover something worthwhile and safely find a way out. Then, suddenly out of the darkness come high winds and a massive sandstorm. I wonder if it is like this outside the labyrinth too. At first, I try to continue, but this is foolish. I'm blinded, and it hurts. Gushing sand, which I assume is coming from the ground in the labyrinth, or from some other source I can't detect, forces me to stop and immediately lie down on my stomach. I hide my face and try to protect it with my arms. Frantic, I'm then overwhelmed by a sense of terror that perhaps I will be buried alive.

Death by sand! Awful!

When I was young, I always feared something like this happening. And even though you have to be alive to imagine it, this truism does nothing to extinguish the worries of my youth. I wonder if this is a random event or if there's someone or something in particular who's causing it. My impression is that the sand is starting to cover me. I kick my legs and attempt to raise my upper body to get some of the sand off. This is successful for the moment, but I can't tell for how long, as the sand seems to keep building up higher and higher. I don't have much time to decide what to do, so I need to make up my mind fast – stay put and hope the storm stops, or try to make my way around a curve to another part of the labyrinth that will maybe protect me from the sand and wind pouring into the part I am in now. I decide that I should wait it out, since I can't really see, and even if I could find my way to another part of the labyrinth, maybe the sandstorm would be just as bad there. I feel this strong tensional pull between action and patience. Waiting? Waiting? And waiting, for how long escapes me. And then suddenly, the storm subsides. Feeling huge relief, I get up and try to brush myself off. I'm saturated in sand. At least I'm alive, but now I really need to find my way out of here before who knows what happens next. After pulling myself together a bit, I plow on through the labyrinth. This is harder than before because of the thick sand on the ground, but as I turn and twist around in many directions, I finally find myself getting closer to some light up ahead. Maybe this is the way out? Previously, any light has been infrequent and fleeting. This light, however, seems more powerful and lasting. When I finally arrive at the fuller light, my impression is that it glows from within a carved out massive rock room. This must be the center of the labyrinth: There are marble floors, stainless steel walls, and iron cabinets.

Wow!

The space is impressive. I gaze around in awe at a vast abandoned chamber. Eerie. It is equipped with what looks like highly sophisticated surveillance technology. Robots and drones, are all over, some whole and others in pieces, and I see hundreds of computers and cameras on the walls and floor. There is a chair in the middle of the room as if a leader was in charge of directing this immense operation, though its raison d'être is unclear. One thing is clear – this was a hidden and protected site for something important – good or evil I cannot tell. I search further, but don't find anything that explains the existence of this place or why I am here on the planet alone. More important now, I think, is to see if there's an exit out of the labyrinth from this bunker. I dare not try to go back through the maze in fear of getting lost all over again. Looking intently for a way out, I notice a ladder on the far side of the room.

To where?

Not sure, but I have to seriously reflect on the possibility that it may be some kind of exit. I ponder this for I don't know how long and eventually decide to go up the ladder and find out. Here goes. After a long climb up, I get to the top and there's a door like thing on the ceiling that I can slide open and go through. I wonder if this is a good idea. Not sure what I'll find or what will find me if I do it. But since I have no other options, I decide to see. The opening brings me to another level that leads into a tunnel. It looks as if this tunnel goes in one direction, so if I enter it I hope I won't be caught up in another labyrinth. Maybe it will take me back up and out to the streets? Maybe not? I start off and all goes well, but it gets darker and darker as I move away from the opening. It's kinda like when you go from bright light to deep darkness, you can actually feel the dark.

Creepy. Disorienting.

All of a sudden, there appears what looks like three irradiated ghouls twenty meters ahead. Their eyes are like shinning black and they wear hooded robes white as snow. Sends shivers down my spine. I don't know what to do. Turn back or keep going? Are they guards of the chamber below? Will I be allowed to pass? These types of apparitions confront me with the highly problematic question of good and evil and thus trust and suspicion. I'm perplexed. I'm getting desperate to get out of here and return to the library and the "possible worlds" of books. I say to myself, just move forward a step at a time and see what happens. As I get closer and closer to the ghouls, they come rushing towards me with a whoosh and knock me over, but then just keep going. I see them sort of flowing through the ceiling door and down into the chamber. Phew! I don't want to stick around for fear that they will come back and do me harm, so I get up on my feet and quickly head on through the tunnel. Unfortunately, at this moment my shoes fall completely apart and I'm too paranoid to stop and check them out. Barefoot it is. Rushing on, I have a side thought – what's preoccupying the ghouls? They'll be coming for me soon, unless maybe they just vanished.

Who knows?

The tunnel now heads upwards. I'm getting really tired, but suddenly I'm at the end and can go no further. Above me there's a small steel door with sort of a steering wheel on it. I'm hoping this is an exit. I turn the wheel and the double plated door opens and I can climb out. I immediately see the streets and realize I'm finally free from the ordeal in the labyrinth. I promise myself never to do anything like that again. What a nightmare!

Dazed and confused as to where I am, I need to find my way back to the labyrinth entry in order to get my bearings and locate the purple markers that will lead me home to the library. I instantly notice that it's now scorching hot again and that the stench, which I couldn't smell as much in the labyrinth, is as strong as ever. But my first priority now is to find some shoes. Covering ground is more arduous than usual. Carefully walking over, around, and through the wreckage is really tough going and soon I feel a bit defeated. I sit and try to concentrate. Where would I be likely to find shoes? I might find some in the remains of a block of collapsed apartment modules or perhaps in a store. But everything looks pretty much the same; it's hard to tell in advance what location could be more promising than another. The huge piles of debris make things difficult to distinguish and I need to get pretty close to see anything. I get up and carry on. I veer to the right and then back to the left, keeping an eye out for the labyrinth entry, while also searching for shoes. Eventually, how long I'll never know, I come upon what appears to be some kind of destroyed habitation for homo and/or techno-sapiens. There are heaps of clothes and fragments of furniture and appliances strewn around, which seems to indicate more human like living environments. After cautiously uncovering rubble piece by piece, I finally find a shoe, and later another; a left and a right, but not alike. One is green and the other blue. Who cares? Sneakers are sneakers. They're a bit damaged, but fit ok and they'll have to do for now. This is a huge relief and allows me to move around faster than with bare feet. I can now devote my attention to finding the labyrinth entry. As I search, it dawns on me that I need to get up higher, so that I can see farther and get a better perspective. When I finally locate a partially standing building, it is starting to get dark and I'm getting paranoid about having to stay somewhere outside the library. I quickly climb up a dangling stairway that clings to the side of the building, though almost fall through a missing step, but I get to a point where I now see off in the distance the oval shaped entry into the labyrinth. Prudently, I head back down the stairs and hope I remember how to get there. Memory is a tricky dimension of my primate life and requires a fine tuned imagination. Back on street level, perception turns out to be more complicated, but memory serves me well, and I'm able to wind my way through the obstacles and eventually find the spot where I placed my last purple marker.

Wow!

Glancing over at the labyrinth entry gives me the creeps, so I'm even more motivated to get out of here. If I can cover ground quickly enough I should be able to make it back to the library before it's completely dark. But I can't move too fast because recklessness could have dire consequences. The terrain is like a blasted minefield. I'm also fearful that with the fading light, I won't be able to detect my purple markers and end up who knows where.

So, off I go.

Fortunately, I still have enough light to see for now. I'm hoping for fairly stable footing as I move as rapidly as I can through the wreckage. I start out a bit too fast and almost twist my ankle, which means I ought to slow down some, even with a decent pair of shoes. When I find a good and steady pace, I make progress and get closer and closer to the library – home. It's so hot I'm sweating profusely. There can't be many purple markers left to find. Then, like out of nowhere, the ghouls show up or in the waning light something that looks like them. Maybe they followed me from the labyrinth, but I didn't see them then, and am I really seeing them now? Difficult to say, but it does seem like three silhouettes there. I'm stunned and scared, but hold my ground.

What's next?

Having to make decisions like this is painful, but I don't have many options. I've got to go on to find the next purple marker. As I continue, the light changes taking a darker tone, but I don't see any ghoulish threats. I reach another marker and soon after another one and then I'm there, back at the library – home.

After spinning around in that labyrinth for who knows how long, weathering the sandstorm and one of my greatest fears of being buried alive, discovering the abandoned chamber, encountering the ghouls, and then having to trek back home in the increasing darkness, leaves me emotionally spent and physically exhausted. I need to eat and drink something and to chill for a while. Regaining some sense of equilibrium after these distressing encounters is no easy task. After I eat and drink, it is now completely dark. I guess I should try to sleep. I'm not sure how wired I am. And the heat is overwhelming. Both these factors, make it difficult for me to get to sleep. The deregulation of the climate on planet Earth with these radical swings from excessive heat to extreme cold, made it no doubt almost impossible for primates like me or much of anything else to survive. With these gloomy thoughts, I toss and turn for some time, how long I'll never know, and then must have gradually drifted into a deep sleep.

When I awake it is light, so I must have slept straight through. Slowly clearing brain fog unveils a dream I had. The marvel of memory and imagination kick in. I recall that I dreamt about two sisters who were co-chief executives of a federation that fought corruption in all sectors of society. They had met with phenomenal success and had thousands of advocates and followers, but were nevertheless under constant pressure from powerful sources who aimed to undermine their efforts and even get rid of them. The balance between justice and injustice was delicate and fragile, but at least justice had held its own. Horrendously, it all changed at this point and the scales tipped strongly in the direction of injustice, which now had a stranglehold in this post-truth world. Injustice prevailed at an alarming pace. When this happened, all went downhill very quickly. I then saw these two heroic sisters, exploitation busters, sitting in a sealed space vehicle transporter and conversing, but I couldn't hear what they're saying. I vaguely made out gestures and facial expressions of taking off, departing, but no sounds. Maybe you know how it is, in some dreams you try and try to do something and don't succeed. You have no control and are susceptible to the dream state, which is actually pretty wonderfully weird when you think about it. Sadly, I was unable to ask them to let me in on the discussion. This was frustrating. I wondered if they were given an ultimatum by the unjust power brokers. Stay on Earth and stop their investigations or continue their activities and be killed. Maybe they had evidence of some massive corruption and wouldn't ever be able to reveal it? Better then to depart and continue to fight for justice, than to capitulate or die. But what influence might they possibly have on Earth from an external location? Where could they go and would they survive the voyage? I had no idea. The next thing I knew, they were gone, vanishing like a shooting star in the sky. Wow! This is probably what woke me. I ponder the dream and how in some ways it seems to reflect a world I remember before whatever happened to leave me alone. How did a world where justice mattered become one in which it was irrelevant? What might this have to do with the destruction all around me? I took some time to process these questions, how long I'll never know.

Eventually, I get up and do a few exercises. Still too hot. I'm sweating. I eat and drink and then meander around gathering more books. When I return to my desk and get things organized a bit, it seems like a good idea to stay put in the library today and read. I look at a few books and

then pick up another collection of poetry. I read a poem written by
James Whitcomb Riley.

We must get home! How could we stray like this?—
So far from home, we know not where it is,—
Only in some fair, apple-blossomy place
Of children's faces—and the mother's face—
We dimly dream it, till the vision clears
Even in the eyes of fancy, glad with tears.

We must get home—for we have been away
So long, it seems forever and a day!
And O so very homesick we have grown,
The laughter of the world is like a moan
In our tired hearing, and its song as vain,—
We must get home—we must get home again!

We must get home! With heart and soul we yearn
To find the long-lost pathway, and return!...
The child's shout lifted from the questing band
Of old folk, faring weary, hand in hand,
But faces brightening, as if clouds at last
Were showering sunshine on us as we passed.

We must get home: It hurts so staying here,
Where fond hearts must be wept out tear by tear,
And where to wear wet lashes means, at best,
When most our lack, the least our hope of rest—
When most our need of joy, the more our pain—
We must get home—we must get home again!

This poem strikes a scintillating chord. It's splendid and compelling.

Sublime! Home!

What a wonderful metaphor and so totally loaded with a surplus of meaning. I think of all the delightful connections to home: Being home; Going Home; Coming Home; Missing Home. I remember home. This poem helps me discover that behind the walls of emotion and the windows of sensation I'm currently experiencing, I desperately long to 'get home.' Home used to be a comfortable imaginative space and far more than merely a physical place. I deeply miss it. Home! It sinks into your flesh and bones becoming part of everyday living in the world. Think of the colors; reds, greens, blues, yellows and the textures; hard, soft, smooth. These are aspects of home, amongst a diversity of others, which generate feelings of calm and serenity. But one of the things that makes home really special is the presence of others: who contribute to making an environment, an atmosphere for being oneself as another. This remarkable configuration, so profoundly integrated into the poetry, brought home to a new level. It goes beyond a geographical location of bricks and mortar to a personal agency of relational significance with the other.

So, one fascinating dimension of home is the connection to others within a family, but also outside it. Self and other had been a much debated topic in many circles, including ethics, philosophy, and psychology, and I remember deep discussions about this with relatives and friends, some of which now come to mind. For all too long the other had been merely seen as a product of the self, which meant that in some way, the other had no 'real' existence apart from its representation by a self. But then, and rightly so, the direction changed. The other started to take primacy over the self. One of the effects of this was to raise the level of ethics from being peripheral, to being central. Other people are not products of one's own making, but they are first of all selves who deserve to be treated with justice and respect. Even though this was a valuable and important shift, it ended up crushing the self. So, this meant there were two extremes or poles: self without other and then other without self. But a better configuration emerged: Oneself as another, which means that neither is canceled out. A different way of saying this is that self and other are related and distinct in tension. Each person deserves and requires a place. In returning to reflect on home I thought: Being home is deeply connected to an appropriate understanding and explanation of both self and other. Thus, among the various meanings of home this is surely a vital one. These memories and thoughts evoked by the poem help me imagine and re-envision the past, which is always with me as I head into the present and then further into the future, though the latter two are still very much a question mark, since I have no idea what might happen next. At any rate, home for me is now the library and the authors, poems, and stories I read, which provide a rich and varied, yet limited context, for a space and place to be in dialogue with self and other – oneself as another.

When I put the book of poems down, I sort of drift off into an imaginative daydream type state, which sends me into a "possible world" of galactic adventures. Sailing through the sky in a fully equipped spacecraft enables me to travel to far off destinations at enormous speeds. These explorations into new frontiers are a monumental challenge, but they might lead me to others who could perhaps help me understand what happened. But maybe I won't find any other primates like me; maybe no earthlings escaped the impending collapse and all died on planet Earth. Who knows? Yet, I still might be able to discover other "informers." My space craft is programed to land on planet X and deftly does so.

Remarkable!

After intensely exploring a few caves and walking up and down gently rolling reddish hills, I come to a place that looks like an enchanted palace. Magnificent twirling golden spires extend high into the sky. The outside is painted a captivating emerald green and manganese violet. There are colorful zip lights hanging all over that brightly illuminate the palace and its delightful architecture of picturesque balconies and quaint inset windows and doors. Looks very tastefully built, but I wonder by who? Were there or are there humans here? I'm longing for real substantial contact with other human primates, a desire for home. In one way or another, for better or worse, this seemed to be how humans evolved. Fascinated by this imaginative prospect, which is having an all-together mesmerizing effect on me, I attentively make my way around the palace, and find an entry. I hesitate about whether or not to go in. I'm cautious because while this place appears enchanting, for all I know it might be haunted. But I feel curious and almost obliged to check it out and see if anyone's home, so I enter through the open shimmering black Iron Gate and massive white wooden door and into the palace. Once inside what I see blows my mind. This place is magic. The sparkling colors on the walls and ceiling are uncanny; yellows, oranges, reds, blues, and greens. It's something like walking into a psychedelic spacesphere that lends itself to hallucinations. Blending and unblending, swirling and unswirling. This gigantic foyer I find myself in has rooms off to the left and right, a long hallway, and several wide spiral paisley staircases that probably lead to upper floors. I go into the room on the right and find a colorful display on the walls and ceiling, but nothing else. It's the same thing in the room on the left. Back in the foyer it strikes me that the color patterns in the two rooms are identical to the ones here. I wonder if they are more than just stunning colors.

A code? A message?

Nothing I can make out for now anyway. I decide to head down the long hall and find dozens of other rooms, which are all exactly the same. Returning from the hall to the foyer, after how long I'll never know, the floor begins to move back and forth and the walls up and down. There's a strange kind of creaking sound. Now I'm getting scared. As much as I enjoyed being pulled into this vortex of colors, this quaking and shaking are too weird. I think I should probably get out of the palace and turn to the door and gate when all of a sudden the whole place disintegrates and I'm left standing with nothing but the dust and dirt of planet X under my feet.

Wow! That was startling. What happened?

I'm sorry the palace is gone and that I never made it to the upper floors to see what was there. I sit down and try to figure out if there's any meaning to take away from this bizarre experience, and this is what comes to me. The identical color patterns in the enchanted palace showed clear signs of perceptive and precise creativity, so perhaps humans had been here at some point, but then maybe the palace was just zapped into existence the same way it was zapped out. Even so, it would still have been a creative endeavor, though produced in a very different way. Someone or something with advanced powers and tech skills may have done this and been observing my explorations in the palace, and just before I went to the upper floors, decided for some reason to pull the plug. But why? What might have been up there? Clues to the destruction of Earth or simply more luring enchantment? Well, whatever the case, it's a mystery and beyond my scope of knowing at this time. I then make my way to the space vessel and head off to planet Earth. Back in the library, as it were, I sort of shake myself out of daydreaming mode and reflect on this strange trip. I think to myself, it would maybe be great to get off Earth and see if there is other life somewhere. Someone or something might be out there, but I have no idea how to actually reach them. At any rate, I'm again amazed at how dreams and imagination allow me to be in two places at the same time. I can be in the library and on Planet X. Here and there – there and here.

Wow!

This dual agency that primates like me have is probably both integrated into our brains and genes and partially a product of culture and environment. But then I reflect, the power of imagination, if left to itself might also be a dangerous weapon in the hands of those with devious intentions. Other "informers" are also necessary. Well, now I better get up and move around some, before I start reading another book. I need to get some physical and mental energy flowing. Feels like I'm running low, so want to replenish. Vitality is an essential, especially in my circumstances, which lend themselves to high degrees of stress.

After refilling, the next story I read is rather short. It is about a wandering nomad who left family, home, and college to move around from place to place, taking work here and there when necessary. Jake took off and left his daily life, to try to bury his past. He went looking for something, but was not sure what. When he met people on the road, which he did when he sometimes hitched a ride or took a bus to another location, they would often ask him what he was looking for as he drifted around. He was never sure how to respond and after these encounters had to think through what he was doing and what, if anything, he wanted to find: a hidden secret, inner peace, harmony with nature, a relationship, love, truth, or a measure of all, or who knows perhaps a myriad of other possibilities. His father, it turns out, influenced his departure.

Jake thought of his mother as easy going and supportive, but he saw his father as an untrustworthy liar. He remembered how his dad had abused him. No one else knew about this and the shroud of silence, at his father's authoritative demand, hung over the sordid affair for many years. It only happened a few times, though for it to have happened at all was devastating and destructive. Jake suffered greatly; a sense of neglect and self-contempt were just two of many unfortunate consequences he had to wrestle with. His father was also a perfectionist and Jake's self-appointed business manager. This included trivial things like calling him out after he had cut the grass at a church and happened to leave a bit on the walkway, or when he insisted that Jake make sure that he collected the money for delivering the newspapers on his paper route by the 10th of every month. Of course none of the money he made could be spent, but had to be saved, not because his parents had no money, but because for his dad "savings" was set in stone. Later in high-school and college Jake became a star basketball player and his dad would attend every game and sort of coach Jake from the sidelines. He'd be thrilled when the team won and Jake had done well, but upset with a loss and critical of Jake for his play. His dad would belittle him and tell him he had to improve. This eventually became all too much for Jake and he decided to quit basketball, shave his head, and take the role of a magician in the school play. He thoroughly enjoyed this new enterprise. It was hard work, but also freeing and the art of magic became a passion for life. His father was shocked and freaked out by Jake's decision. He told Jake he could never understand him. Why would he give up the possibility of making millions from sports? What would the neighbors and the school think? His father accused him of bringing shame and disgrace to his family, though what he really meant was to himself. At this point, it was all about his dad and his demands, and the perverse lies he told to cover up his abuse. Jake decided he could care less. Jake's father eventually confessed to him that he had mental health issues and was seeing a psychiatrist for depression and psychological problems. This was the last time Jake saw him.

During the years of his nomadic travel Jake worked for and talked with hundreds of people. Through these encounters he learned a lot about them and about himself. Before leaving one place for another, Jake got in the habit of stopping at the end of a lane to contemplate his life. He'd sit for hours wondering, reminiscing, and questioning who he was and what the world was all about. Then in one town he was passing through, a circus came to perform for five nights. Jake went to every show and thoroughly enjoyed each performance. As the circus was packing up, he asked if he could travel with it. The answer was yes. So, Jake joined the circus troupe for two years and during that time trained to be a magician, his passion that began way back in his college days. After his training, he became a full time magician and continued touring with the circus for a few years. In one sense, he had found a moveable home among the homeless. Eventually, Jake quit the circus and then again travelled around on his own. He spent time helping the homeless find a home, cheering children in hospitals, and bringing joy to seniors in care giving establishments. For him these encounters were like home, and he continued to embrace them as he went on.

This is an intriguing story. Jake's father and his actions are clearly part of the tragedy of this narrative. Even though Jake and his father are fictional characters, I still grieve for what happened to Jake.

Horrible.

I remember my previous reflections and the stunning poem about home that I read in the library earlier. It's sad that Jake was deprived of home in one sense, though encouraging that he found it in another. But I'm blown by what Jake still achieved in spite of his circumstances. He had tremendous strength and courage to deal with his situation; to seal off parts of his past and attempt to leave them behind, and to become a nomad roaming around hoping to find something of a "possible world."

Wonderful!

His choice to follow a passion and become a magician was remarkable. He brought incredible joy to hundreds and hundreds of people. And I marveled how in each location of his travels, he stopped at the end of the road and pondered the meaning of life.

After taking a break, I then pick up a massive book about ancient Greece and leaf through it. A different kind of story, but fascinating. In this period, according to human historiography, there was an outpouring of literature, including provocative myths, challenging poetry, innovative plays, and magisterial epics. Philosophy, political systems, science, and architecture also advanced to new levels, and it is clear that these evolving Homo sapiens left their mark on the Earth in many ways, perhaps for better or worse. Intriguingly, the weight of superstition and the fear of the gods were prominent in these days of wars, chaos, and calamity. There were high levels of suspicion concerning features of the natural world that to them seemed threatening and scary. Territorial issues were monumental as food and other resources meant survival, and survival was dependent on being able to defend yourself, your clan, and your land. Yet, survival was such a treacherous task. One never knew if the gods were on one's side or not. They were assumed to be capricious and deceitful, and believed to have massive power and ultimate control. They exercised this power at the whims of their own will and for their own well-being, disregarding the needs of desperate human primates who were demanded to offer sacrifices, including sometimes one of their own. The most famous and strongest gods had the wily ability to start and fight wars, sometimes against each other scheming to establish dominion and be the main god of the gods, other times inciting tribe against tribe, Queen against Queen, King against King in order to gain an advantage for their own selfish purposes. Some of this was recounted in the great epics of Homer and through the fascinating dialogues of the philosophers, including Socrates, Plato, and Aristotle. I realize the influence of this literature and these thinkers was formidable and that people had debated about and benefitted from such extraordinary resources for centuries.

I will probably keep this book nearby, so I can read more later. The Greeks were amazing. I learned a lot from this tome, but was particularly struck by the beliefs in the gods and the levels of superstition about the natural world. This is so strikingly different from nowadays, where the gods have all but disappeared and nature is seen as an intricate machine that runs on its own. Modern people tended to believe the world was stable and safe, but its present condition now seems to be far from that. Who had the better view? Well, probably neither.

Hard to say.

After reading all day, I get up and walk around a little. It is still sweltering and there's no breeze, but I need a bit of exercise. So hot – these hot and cold extremes remain puzzling. Weather patterns had been deregulated for ages by climate change, but this seems to be worse. The light is fading and it will soon be dark. Time to sleep. Turns out this is difficult, even though I'm pretty tired. Eventually, I doze off, but you know how it is when you have one of those sleeps where you're actually not sure you really slept, yet you must have. At any rate, it was something like that.

Venturing out of the library the following morning with a sense of renewed energy, I want to try to take my search a bit further than on some of my previous sorties. Bringing along a bunch of black rags for markers I set off to the north. Today is another gray day. Seems like most days are like this, whether it's hot or cold. This may be due to the high levels of pollution hanging over planet Earth. After slogging on through the wasteland, for how long I'll never know, I see what appears to be a half erect building sticking out of the flattened wreckage. When I duck in through an overhang like structure and look around, I see what I have found in a few other places of this kind: thousands of data type super computers shredded into shards. There are also remnants of desks and chairs, fragments of storage containers, pieces of stainless steel vaults, and security cameras, some still attached to the walls and others dangling or on the ground. Looks like another high level info tech center that was maybe also processing and storing documents. I eventually discover piles of blank paper, perhaps awaiting a large amount of data to come through, but I guess that never happened, as least as far as I can tell. Then I find three pages of printed out digital codes, or something like that, which surprisingly are still in pretty good condition. As I look at them, it becomes clear to me that I won't be able to decipher anything without a code breaker key; a de-coder to interpret the coded symbols and graphics. Perhaps, these pages were the last of millions that passed through here. Something important as some sort of ending or final communication may turn up. But maybe there's nothing relevant in them.

Who knows?

If I can locate a master Cyber slider - Crypto vipteo, I'll be in business. A Cyber slider - Crypto vipteo is a double sided complex device that is able to decipher and interpret coded documents almost as fast as they are produced. Even though this will be like trying to find a needle in a haystack amidst all the wreckage, it's worth a go. The search is on. I start near the pile of blank pages since this is where the 'interpreter' most likely would be used for incoming messages. As the data was churned out, someone had to decode it. This type of position tended to be held by techno-sapiens, privileged over mere humans due to their efficiency and discretion. Techno-sapiens had the capacity to deal with huge amounts of material and then make it available without exploitation. As programmed agents they typically obeyed and could almost always be trusted to keep security matters private. My pursuit of the code breaker continues. I uncover layers and layers of rubble, but don't find anything. I move a meter from where I started and search there. After tossing away a pile of computer pieces, I see a safe or strong box attached to the ripped up floor. This might be just the sort of place the 'interpreter' would be stored when not in use, though it might also be a location for top secret confidential material of a third kind. At any rate, whatever might be in there, it would be interesting to see what's inside. Unfortunately, the safe couldn't be opened digitally and there was no card key ready at hand.

I then am startled by a loud noise; kind of like the sound of a blast and as I gazed up and out, there is an eruption of colors that is absolutely splendid – reminded me of a Kandinsky painting. He tended to use vivid colors and to weave them together in such a remarkable fashion resembling what I now had in front of my eyes. After this brilliant display sort of wafted away, a mercurial figure appeared as if 'out of the blast.' This blinking filmy like colorful substance had no corporeal features, but only a presence of about one square meter in space, and it is moving from side to side or up and down within a limited range. Seems as if these movements are programmed and the thing may be a disguised covert robot or master drone of some kind, sent by someone or something. And so I suddenly wonder if I was being blatantly and openly watched and if so by whom and for what? For all I know, my appearing to be alone in the world might be an experiment by some form of superior intelligence. Or maybe, I'm going to get a revelation – a message – a clue from an unknown source about how to open the safe? I stand my ground sort of mesmerized by this thing, until it suddenly soars off into space and disappeared.

Not sure what that was about, but now I should focus on trying to get into the safe. I spend a fair amount of energy on this, but eventually realize that my lame efforts are no match for this sophisticated device. In other words, I'm unsuccessful. Since the safe is not opening, I will continue my search for the Cyber slider - Crypto vipteo elsewhere. When I get up, I look back over my right shoulder. I see several Golden statuettes, perhaps from ancient times, dangling from the partially standing wall. Attracted by these glittering figures, I move closer to get a better look. As I do so, I suddenly become aware that these statuettes are not ancient relics after all. It appears that they are something like contemporary awards for outstanding performances perhaps given to those who ran this data center, or whatever it was. But nothing indicates who was giving these prizes or why. What power(s) were in a position to acknowledge excellence and reward it with something like this?

My thoughts drift off in this direction, but I am left with an open deck concerning this question and must leave it for later. For now I need to keep looking for the decoder. I immerse myself in the task at hand hoping for success, however, in spite of my efforts, contending with the mess under and around me becomes impossible. There's just too much stuff. The more I uncover, the more piles up right next to it, and then I have to un-pile that and this creates another pile. Hyper disappointing. So, the search is beginning to feel like – well, futile, and the likelihood that I'll find the Cyber slider - Crypto vipteo to decode the three pages seems ultra slim.

I reluctantly give up and start to leave the damaged building, but on the way out I bang my head on a hanging beam. In my next fully conscious moment, I find myself sprawled on the ground with a gash on my forehead, and have no idea of how long I've been lying here. Momentarily zonked, I guess. I'm still kinda dazed and confused. As I slowly come to my senses, I remember a weird trip I had while in my half-conscious state or whatever it was. It seemed like an out of body experience where I was taken by winged beings of some sort to a mysterious location. A wispy thin cloud covered the night sky, but allowed a zillion stars to shine through. This billowing form of dark and lighter grays shrouded the horizon and appeared to resemble a host of creatures: unicorns, griffins, and dragons choreographed into the clouds. Then the clouds parted and I saw green fields and vineyards, a forest of oaks, redwoods, sequoias, and snow-capped mountains with rushing water. An unbelievably beautiful piano solo resonated as a phantom opened a massive door to a vast empty space. But in the blink of an eye the space was filled by a wall made up of thousands of small colorful squares. The phantom, no doubt a light show artist, smiled a spectral grin, and suddenly these squares lit up with brilliant luminescence, projecting oranges, blues, purples, reds and yellows that were rich, deep, and sharp, like nothing I had ever seen before. At the center of this wall of color, there was a flashing square with an integrated lock. On the right side, almost out of view, there was a gorgeous sealed wooden box. After unsealing it, the phantom took out a small brass key, and placed it in the lock, but did not turn it. On the left side, also barely visible, was an altar like piece adorned with silver winged animals and what looked like gold and precious jewels. Several large royal eagles and a gigantic gypaète barbu (French for lammergeier) soared above it. Two gleaming goblets were set on the altar piece. This appeared to be a sacrificial scene for some kind of sacred ritual. The phantom raised the first goblet and put it back on the altar, and after doing the same with the second one, it vanished. I was perplexed and wondered what this is all about.

Was this a real altar?
What kind of ceremony, if any, was taking place?
What was in the goblets?
Why were they raised?
To whom, if anybody?

I have no idea and was given no clue. Then, the brass key began to jiggle in the lock. It occurred to me that someone or something should turn the key to find out what was inside this flashing square. But then I wondered if that would be a good idea or not.

Who knows what was in there?

Just then the enormous gypaète barbu flew in closer and closer. It was incredibly fast and agile for such a big bird. Swooping in it took a sharp right then left turn and latched onto the key with its strong beak. At first the key seemed to resist, but the powerful bird finally turned it and the flashing square quit flashing and opened. For a moment nothing happened. But all of a sudden, a great force from inside the opening seemed to pull the bird through the now enlarged square and into the vortex of outer space, where it disappeared. Then I watched in dismay, as one by one the other birds were also sucked into oblivion.

Wow! This was terrifying.

I feared now I would be next and held on for dear life, but the pulling sensation abruptly ceased and everything was calm. I immediately noticed that the square with the integrated lock was flashing again. The wall looked exactly as it did previously, except that the brass key was already in the lock. I wondered if what had just happened would repeat itself over and over. And sure enough the phantom reappeared, but this time without any sacrificial paraphernalia. As it readied itself to turn the key and open the flashing square, I was paranoid and my disembodied presence was on high stress alert. After the phantom finally turned the key and opened the square, it vanished, and nothing happened. I awaited the mighty pulling sensation, but it didn't come. However, this time the Cyber slider - Crypto vipteo floated out of the square. It was hand-held in size, and was sparkled with cadmium orange and cerulean blue. Stunned and excited, I desperately wanted to reach for the decoder, but couldn't move. I wondered where the three pages of codes were. Maybe they were coming too? Maybe not? If I could only grab the Cyber slider - Crypto vipteo. Alas, the pages never arrived. And then to my horror the decoder sailed back into the square and the phantom returned, took the key out of the lock and threw it into the air, and then the whole colorful wall dissolved. Wall and decoder, gone.

At this point, I must have begun to recover more of my senses because I can't remember anything else about this time - space I appear to have been in after hitting my head. I'm happy to have my body back, but my head is pounding. I sit and ponder this experience, wondering if it is more than just a dream. It would have been fantastic to have that Cyber slider - Crypto vipteo. I'm so intrigued by what might be hidden in the codes, but I imagine now I'll never find out.

Who knows?

I get up, wipe the dried blood off my head, and carefully make my way through the ruins and back out of the partly standing building. Phew! From what I can tell from my previous journeys outside the library, there might have been thousands of these types of places. Data, Data and more Data. Surveillance, Surveillance, and more Surveillance. Deception, Deception, and more Deception. This seems to be all that the "powers" were interested in before the world exploded or whatever happened to it. I imagine that as the digital world became the template for reality or maybe even replaced it, a massive amount of technology was required to maintain control of primate like me populations, until they were either destroyed, shipped off to another location, or altered into techno-sapiens who would offer little resistance to power brokers.

I guess I have traveled further than I thought since when I look I have no markers left. Walking back and forth, I eventually spot what must be the last marker I planted, so now I have a direction. As I start back, a little wobbly at first, to the library and its books full of stunning worlds, I reflect on this horrible debacle and wonder again what's going on. My progress is not very fast, but I grind on finding the markers as I go. After some time, who knows how long, I realize that I haven't seen any black markers for a while now. This startles me some and my of anxiety spikes. I think to myself, maybe I'm lost. The fear of getting lost is something that continually haunts me. Not sure why? Perhaps, I should retrace my steps and see if I can locate the previous marker. But this will be difficult because so much of the terrain looks the same, which makes direction confusing. I ask myself, well, if I decide to go back, how far back should I go? If I risk turning around, I may get further off course than I already am. The sky darkens and the ominous gray clouds are dipping lower.

I'm so wired up by what's happening that it's hard to calm down and sort this out carefully. The thought of it being dark soon crosses my mind. This will certainly make it complicated to see any markers, and finding the library again will be next to impossible. Then an even more distressing thought comes to me, and I wonder if someone or something has removed them. Well, I'm probably not going to figure that one out now, so I better refocus on the task at hand. I sit down on a pile of debris and try to imagine where I last saw a marker. I usually put them close enough to each other so this kind of thing doesn't happen. So, I imaginatively go back to the partly standing building where I searched for the Cyber slider - Crypto vipteo and banged my head. I marvel at how my imaginative memory is again helping me be in two places at once, from the pile of debris here, I envision the setting back there.

I remember now that the last marker I saw was stuck into a heap of red bricks, which I recall thinking at the time was unusual as I had not seen any of these during my previous journeys. So, that's a good indication. I need now to work back to this location and if it's still there I will hopefully be able to see the one that I previously missed. Back I go.

Fortunately, I discover a bunch of old metal spikes that I can use as new markers, so if I go the wrong way I can at least find my way back here, and if necessary head off in another direction in hopes of finding the red bricks. Trying to recognize where I came from isn't easy. It's all so similar: flattened houses and buildings with rubble strewn all over. After going in one direction for a spell, I don't find any red bricks, so I figure I'll go back and head out in another direction. I do wonder though if I have gone far enough to really be sure this is not the right way.

Who knows?

But I guess it's better to go shorter distances to begin with and be able to quickly return to my starting point, if I don't find anything, and try other possible routes. So, I'm now back to where I started. Suddenly, my body trembles. I look around and see everything is shaking. An Earthquake! Wow, this is incredible. Stuff is moving all over big time. I dive to the ground, but then think, I hope the ground beneath me doesn't split open and swallow me up. Seems like the trembling goes on forever, but actually as quick as it started, the quake now stops.

I remember experiencing earthquakes and hiding under a school desk or standing in a doorway when I was younger. My town was prone to earthquakes.

This one freaked me out.

I lie there for some time, how long I'll never know, and eventually get up to survey the landscape. Sure enough, cracks up to a meter wide split the ground and a fair amount of debris has disappeared into them. Phew! The quake must have been massive. I really didn't have anything to hold on to as the Earth was shaking and this thought leaves me feeling even more vulnerable. Sort of hollow inside.

I need to move on now in a new direction. Hopefully, there won't be any strong aftershocks and the pile of red bricks has not been swallowed up into the Earth. To find my bearings would be a huge relief, but getting from one place to the next is even more challenging with the gaping crevices. I have to be careful, but must also hurry, while I still have the light. After a spell, having not found the bricks I go back to the starting point. I feel a few tremors, but nothing too serious. So, I head in another direction. As I'm yet again unsuccessful, I'm just about to turn back when all of a sudden, a hot southerly wind blows, le foehn, as it is called in some parts of the world, and with it comes a carnival-esque figure wearing a colorful costume and wild mask, as people in some countries used to do in the old days to chase away the spirits of darkness and winter. The costume is incredible: deep purple pants – baggy and wavy, and a loose yellow shirt with flowing tassels of blue, red, and orange. The mask is frightening: black and gray, with a menacing grin. This character doesn't seem to be a person and looks more like a puppet, but without strings. What kind of strange manifestation is this? It seems to have come out of nowhere and floats in the air about ten meters away for me. I wonder, as I have several times previously, if this is my projection or perhaps someone else's. Might not be either.

At any rate, this puppet like figure seems to be pointing in the direction I just turned back from, wanting me to continue further on. Why? Is this is a trap of some kind? Should I trust this apparition or be suspicious of it? Puppets, like clowns, tend to be either benevolent or mischievous, and at times both. There it is again: trust and suspicion playing central roles in life decisions. I have to decide, and even though I'd like more time for reflection, the light is fading, and I need to make up my mind quickly. Ok, I'll go farther in that direction and see what happens. As I forge on, I see that the floating costume and mask is also moving keeping a step ahead of me as I go. When I come to a huge split in the ground I veer to the right, and as I do, there about thirty meters away are the pile of red bricks! Phew! As I reach the bricks, the puppet like figure vanishes.

Without the apparition, I may not have found the marker, so for this time anyway, trust was the better option. I can't reflect any longer on this episode, as I have to try to figure out where I went wrong before and get back on the path to the library. But after the quake, the marker might have changed position. Scanning left and then right I can't detect anything. I move ahead five meters, and there it is off in the distance. I must have not been paying attention when I got off track the first time, or maybe banging my head affected my concentration and I strayed off course without realizing it. At any rate, finding the marker is an enormous relief, though there's no time to celebrate. I need to keep focused now and hurry back as darkness sets in and the clouds sweep in lower. Light is fading fast, and I don't want to have to spend the night outside the library. Climbing over debris and now more wreckage due to the huge earthquake is arduous. I feel another tremor, it shakes stuff around some, but then stops. Further on I see the next marker, so I'm going in the right direction. This is good news. I'm encouraged that I'm definitely making progress and that there has been no strong aftershocks, though I'm still worried about losing light or having an encounter with who knows what that will prevent or delay me from getting home. There is sweat pouring off me. It's still so hot and I have to work hard to make any headway. I search for the next marker, ah yes, now I see it, but when I get to it, I don't immediately see the next one yet, so head out hesitatingly, without committing myself to any direction. I scramble up pile of shattered blocks of concrete to get a better perspective. From this vantage point, I try to locate the marker, but at first I'm not successful. I'm getting worried. On a second viewing, I think I might barely see it, but have get closer for a better look. Yep, it's good. Some rubble from the earthquake has almost covered it, but I can just make it out. It's now almost dark and with the low gray clouds I'm having problems seeing, but at this point I don't think I can be too far from the library. I spot another marker and another before just being able to make out the contours of the partially standing shelter that I have come to perceive of and to experience as home, then one last marker before finally arriving. Wow! What a wild trip, earthquake, puppet, and all. In this precious moment, I'm thrilled to be back and feel a sense of being sheltered.

I'm really hungry, thirsty, and tired, so I sit at my desk and eat, drink, and rest in the twilight of time, as darkness follows its perpetual rhythm and, slowly but inevitably, closes in on me. Unfortunately, I can't read anything now and will have to wait until the light returns. It seems to have cooled down a bit, so perhaps I can sleep, but you know how it is when you lie down after an intense and adventurous time, then you begin to run through the events of the day sort of processing things as memory and imagination light up the dark space, you can find it hard to sleep. That our wildly complex and intricately complicated human brains play such an essential role, or at least so it seems to me, in sleep motivation or sleep deprivation is indeed mysterious. I eventually doze off, as when I next open my eyes, there is light. Gradually emerging from what I assume is a sleep state, I wonder what it would be like to probe the parameters of life and death as an observer; to stand outside these related yet distinct phenomena and 'see' them for what they are. But of course that could never be a 'real' possibility.

After kind of side-stepping that thought, I remember several dreams I had. In the first dream, if I recall correctly, four women were accused of an act of sedition against the Empire authorities, and were put in prison. I didn't know these ladies, but thought of them as the fearless four. It was almost as if they wanted to be arrested, so they could fight and hopefully win a court battle for themselves and others who sought to be free from unjust power structures and devious despots. They awaited the chance to make a defense before a judge. Other prisoners roamed around in a large cell that was sort of smoky or cloudy, while the fearless four were kept in a smaller cell of their own. I couldn't see any faces, but felt their presence. When the day finally came after several postponements, the fearless four, acted as their own defense and what a defense it was. Absolutely brilliant. All accusations were deftly refuted, but at the last minute the prosecution produced a witness that falsely claimed to have infiltrated the four and testified that they had indeed planned to overthrow the Empire. On these dubious grounds, the judge pronounced them guilty and sentenced them to thirty years in a high security prison in the far north. What a disgraceful sham. This was evidence that levels of corruption and injustice had increased exponentially, making it impossible to ever win against the Empire. The fearless four were thoroughly appalled and so was I. The following night while on route to the far off prison the ladies were unchained during a stop and whisked away by a spacecraft, hopefully to be taken to a safe place where they could continue to undermine the Empire, but in the end I was left without a clue concerning their fate. Too bad, but the dream realm or state can be detailed in some areas and murky and inconclusive in others.

My next dream seemed to be located in a vast park or garden; full of trees, grass, flowers and shrubs. There were lots of primates that appeared to look like me, as well as robots, and techno-sapiens, all roaming around. Then suddenly I heard eerie sounds come from what probably were loud speakers. All these beings or pseudo-beings that had been moving in different directions, immediately turned in the same direction, as if programmed, and gathered together on a slight incline that appeared to be in the middle of the park or garden. When they, maybe thousands of them had all arrived they held hands and bowed to someone or something I couldn't see. What happened next was mind blowing. Everyone just disintegrated. Gone. I wasn't sure if they had been "translated" into a different state, or perhaps teleported to another place, or had just disappeared never to reappear. Had they been freed, enslaved, or were they dead?

Who knows?

I was shocked by this - whatever it was - and wanted to get away from this place as fast as possible. But I couldn't move. It was like I was stuck to the ground. And every step I tried to take seemed to lower me further and further down into the earth. I tried to scream for help, however no sound came out of my mouth, at least that I could hear. All of a sudden, a wizard appeared wearing a dazzling black flowing robe and a huge loose fitting hood. I could not see a face, but only shining diamond shaped orange eyes moving back and forth as if scanning something. Instead of performing any magical acts, the wizard just reached out a hand, which looked like it was mangled, and grabbed on to mine pulling me out of the ground. At this juncture, I glanced down at my feet and then up again. The wizard had vanished, and I then faded away from the park or garden.

In the last dream I recall, there were a host of weird creatures crawling out of the water, eerie large winged birds flying around in the sky, and spooky plants popping up from the ground. It looked like some kind of prehistoric setting. Reminded me of a Hieronymus Bosch painting. There was a sense of beauty, but also menace in this strange environment. I felt anxious, as if something dramatic was about to happen. Then a three headed poisonous serpent emerged from a cave searching for prey, but remarkably it turned out it was preyed upon by a massive sabre toothed tiger. An epic battle between them ensued and I wasn't sure who would win or if it mattered, yet for some reason I felt it did. The tiger eventually tore the serpent to shreds and moved off the scene. But somehow the serpent revived, though with only one head. It turned and came straight at me. I totally freaked out and this must have jolted me awake.

Reflecting on these dreams, I find some of their themes, including justice, injustice, determinism, destiny, predator/prey, quite relevant topics to be dreaming about. Dreams are so amazing, but it's hard to know what to make of them. Do they reveal something of who we are? I could spend all day pondering and trying to figure things out. I better let them go for the moment and move on. I get up and eat and drink something. It seems cooler today, so perhaps the freezing weather is coming. I plow through the library uncovering more books and selecting a few to add to my already significant collection. Reading a book is so often much more than just reading, though not less. Other factors play into the art of reading, including mood and atmosphere, energy and fatigue, concentration and day dreaming. I return to my desk and open one book and then another to see if anything stands out at the present time. There seems to be richness and value in them all.

The book I finally decide to read is a story set in a small country. In one region made up of many villages, the majority of those who live here are farmers. These farmers struggled with difficult conditions. Water supplies were meager, the ground was rocky, and the weather often hot and dry. Through hard labor in the fields and at home, the villagers tried to produce enough for their families and sold fruits, vegetables, handmade crafts, and art, at the markets in one of the larger towns to earn a little money.

One farming family, Sylvia and Raymond and their two adult children, decided to start a co-op to manage the resources of the farms and insure that each farmer was treated fairly. The idea was to help the farmers and establish fairness and conditions so that no one would under sell or over produce at the expense of others. Many of the farmers from the surrounding villages gladly joined, but a few were reluctant. This was due to another important reason for founding the co-op, which was political. Sylvia and Raymond hoped to create a unified front of solidarity that would be able to stand against the Governor General and his soldiers, who oppressed the farmers and forced them to pay an outrageously high government tax. This unjust taxation had been going on for years, and no one had any doubt that the Governor was corrupt and greedy. A farmer then took matters into his own hands and killed the Governor, but the irony here, as the narrator pointed out, was that he then became the Governor General himself.

The farmers celebrated his victory and enjoyed their new freedom and all went well for a while. Eventually, things degenerated in the region and many voices raised questions about the new authority and ways of doing things. As a result, and in fear of losing his power the new Governor did something he had promised never to do: he reinstated the old taxes and took away many of the new found freedoms of the farmers: the Oppressed now became the Oppressor. Why does this happen so often? Power can somehow turn into cruelty. None of the farmers openly objected or refused to pay for fear of being beaten or killed. The Governor's new aim now was to keep everyone in line and under control, so when it came to the co-op and its leaders, he made a visit to Sylvia and Raymond to find out their point of view. They boldly stated their reasons for setting up the co-op and requested that the tax be lowered and gradually abolished. The Governor saw this as treason and a political threat to his sovereign rule. Inadmissible. He felt threatened and freaked out. The co-op must cease. If it didn't, the leaders and any who supported them would be beaten and thrown into prison. Sylvia and Raymond had two weeks to disband the co-op and any organized efforts to resist: the Oppressed had indeed become the Oppressor. When the farmers met to discuss this, the exchange of views was lively. Some maintained that it would be best to do things the way they always had done. Just pay the taxes. This would be safer. Others argued that the corruption and injustice had to stop and that if there was no other way they should fight to overthrow the Governor and his troops. This would be riskier, but the only way to gain freedom for present and future generations. Gradually, after more discussion, most agreed to stand against the tyranny of the Governor. But this presented a huge problem. The farmers had no experience in fighting battles. They were not soldiers, and the Governor was very well protected. Sylvia and Raymond, however, had an idea. How about Peaceful resistance? Everyone laughed and no one thought this would work, since real change in power seemed to only come with violence. But Sylvia and Raymond explained that after their meeting with the Governor they had the impression that he was actually beginning to have second thoughts. His transformation from Oppressed to Oppressor had been debilitating and had left him physically and psychologically exhausted and in a constant quandary concerning how best to proceed with the farmers. To resist, albeit peacefully, might put more pressure on him. Finally, all agreed to try this, yet without much conviction that it would work. The hope was that the Governor would break down and regret his corrupt ways and would ultimately resign. If that were ever to happen it certainly would be a first for this region, but it was worth a try. So, the co-op publically disbanded, but the farmers remained unified in peaceful resistance against the Governor. This did not go well at first, and many farmers were beaten and jailed for not paying taxes, including Sylvia and Raymond. Several weeks passed and things worsened. Some began to think that violence was indeed the only way to bring about change. Then, one farmer died as a result of being severely beaten. It turns out that this farmer had previously been the neighbor and friend of the new Governor. The farming community mourned its loss, but his death profoundly affected the Governor to the extent that he finally came to his senses and released all those in prison and then resigned. This was a victory, a bitter one, but still a victory for the farmers. After regaining their strength, Sylvia and Raymond, requested a meeting with all the farmers. Everyone from the region was there. They talked for hours and decided it was time to find a better way of working and living together. They re-started the co-op, so each farmer could get help and advice about shared rights and responsibilities in the community, and this was accepted. During this meeting, they also voted to no longer have a Governor General in order to try to avoid the bad experiences when they had a single leader, and elected Sylvia and Raymond instead as co-coordinators to lead the way forward into a new era of teamwork, built hopefully on trust and integrity. As it turned out, the couple proved to be skillful and wise leaders, and brought about landmark changes that were beneficial to the region for years to come.

I find this story uplifting. The passionate portrayal of these farmers, who in spite of difficult conditions still managed to carve out a life for themselves, is impressive. But their tenacious desire to be free from injustice and corruption is even more stunning and exemplary. The commitment and integrity of Sylvia and Raymond are outstanding. Their insights into humanity, unwavering patience, and daring vision for a new and just community are truly remarkable. I keep coming back to the interplay between the Oppressed and Oppressor, and wondered why sometimes the Oppressed, once freed tended to become Oppressors themselves. This is indeed, for me, a mystery, but at least this story had managed to valiantly break the vicious cycle and end differently.

After I put down the book, I must doze off, as the next thing I know, I wake from a disturbing dream. I was trapped in an empty building and running down the stairs from floor to floor, opening the Exit door on each one only to find that it opened to nothing – taking a step out would be like falling into space. Still hoping that I would eventually find a way out of the building I opened yet another Exit door. And there before me was an alarming apparition; maybe a primate like me, but somehow more ghostly. Aghast, I screamed slurring: Who are you? Who are you? No response. Who are you? No response. I stood there staring at this macabre figure. Then suddenly, someone or something from inside the building tried to pull me back by my legs from the open door, from the nothingness, from the apparition. I couldn't turn to see who or what this was, but for some reason I had the feeling that it was something even more threatening. My fear spiked and I started struggling and kicking as hard as I could to get loose from this terrifying sensation of being pulled towards the depths of the unknown. My legs were still moving as if riding a bike when I snapped out of my dream mode. This dream might have something to do with my present circumstances. Dreams take place in such a weird state and this makes them ultra-difficult to interpret. Well, I find making sense of my waking life already a highly complex undertaking, so trying to understand my dreams is even more complicated, but no doubt still worth reflecting on. Maybe later.

The weather had now turned freezing. I gear up to leave the library and see what I can find out about my current situation. I take a stack of blue markers that I had prepared in case I head into unknown territory. I'm still hoping that one of these days I'll discover something new – a clue or insight – a symbol or image, something more than a hint – that will shed light on what's going on here. I carefully maneuver around several obstacles and carry on up the battered street. The sky is filled with heavy gray clouds and it looks as if it's going to rain or snow, but somehow it never does, at least not here. After a while, how long I'll never know, I turn right into what looks like an alley and start leaving markers to find my way back. I trudge through torn up cobblestones and broken glass, old wood beams and concrete. When I get out of this passageway between larger streets, I find myself in a boulevard – a wide open space. I ramble along and start noticing fragments of big screens lying on the ground. I look around: there are thousands of them, some totally shattered and others in large enough pieces to grab my attention. I explore further and begin to realize that there are also fragments of VR headsets and gaming paraphernalia strewn all over which seems to indicate that this wasn't a typical surveillance center or data processing outfit, like those I had come across previously. In the rubble, I find piles of broken equipment, plates, cups and saucers, along with mattresses and lamps. I wager this must have been one of those huge digital games and adventure palaces with restaurants and hotels that had taken over blocks and blocks of buildings and were open 24/7. These palaces offered the ultimate experience of adventure and the choice of games was almost endless. Since the entire Earth had become so polluted no one did much outside, and these types of places were extremely popular. Primates like me, pseudo-primates, and others could spend hours, sometimes even days on a journey and playing games. Some spent a good part of their lives in these environments without having to leave to eat or sleep. All you had to do was find your thing and plug yourself in for the time of your life. Whatever your current space, you could experience another and another until you could no longer remember where you started from. But I suppose getting lost in space was akin to an adventure in the wild and thus a trip worth taking. Phantom narrators created and told stories that pulled you into the visual vortex of sound, light, color, and motion, that spiked imagination and constructed emotions. Nothing quite like it. Floating from the actual worlds, to the virtual worlds, and then back again was a constant challenge and lure that hooked you into a life of continual adventure and play, and for many this was now the real world – the world to come. Teleportation had become widespread for moving around in limited distances. This made it easy to transition from one digital platform to another in the palaces; from one restaurant to another or one hotel to another. There were also Chatbots located here and there on the massive site. You could enter a soundproof cube and the voice of lost loved ones would speak to you about where they were and how they transitioned from life to death and back to some other form of life again. Perhaps, there really was another dimension of consciousness. I'm not sure, but this seems more akin to tech fabrication, which had become widely acceptable and for many it simply didn't matter anymore.

At this moment, out of the blue, I suddenly remember talking to friends about near death, and out of the body experiences, that we had read about. Some primates like me had visions of looking down on themselves lying in bed, while others saw in the distance a bright light and had a pleasurable sensation that all was well, or they saw their lives flash before them, before rejoining their body. The medical and scientific worlds started to focus in on near death or even post death narratives, where in this latter case someone had been declared dead, but returned to life to tell about it. Long and elaborate studies hoped to figure out specifically how the brain or consciousness (whatever that is) functioned in these extraordinary moments. Memory and imagination also came into play. Locating another sphere of consciousness, which was thought to exist, but which was unattainable in normal circumstances, became a hot spot for funding and sparked widespread interest, as the number of these 'death' stories increased and took on a more frequent character. For all that was known, much remained unknown.

Thinking about it now, it's entirely possible that there is a hidden reality behind things and that had investigations continued, a connection between worlds of consciousness might have been found someday. Wouldn't it be something to find and emerge into a new realm, bodily or otherwise?

Alas, here I still am with all this technology around me in ruins. I just got so carried away by my reflection and imagination about life, death, and reality that I forgot where I was. Marvelous! When I return, so to speak, to matters at hand, the vast amount of debris strikes me yet again. While planet Earth's environment had become toxic, many primates like me and other beings seem to have spent more and more time in these types of attraction parks, which in turn produced a mechanistic alliance with the status quo, rather than an imaginative impulse to change.

Imagination was deceived and even replaced by tech simulation, which had the corrosive effect of a debilitating drug and would eventually lead to death. 'Techemics,' as they called them, were extremely popular, yet devastating. I can't help but wonder if this partially explains what's happened and why I appear to be here alone. Perhaps this site, and probably thousands like it, was one of the factors that contributed to the demise of planet Earth and the de-humanization of humanity. It seemed like technology was useful in so many ways, until it became dominant and controlled by the few. After surveying the landscape one last time, I take my wonderings with me and move on up the road.

As I trudge along, my thoughts are racing and keep leading back to the phenomenon of death. Seems most primates like me didn't want to die. Flesh and blood was our material representation on Earth and we tended to desperately want to hold on to these. Being embodied meant to be alive, to have a space and at least a physical place in the world. We just got used to it, which seems to have been a normal development. Sure, being alive was much more than this, but not less. The lingering fear of being disembodied translated into the devastating anxiety of non-existence. I thought of the dead; the millions and millions of lost relations and then the millions and millions of missing memories. Who could count them?

But here I am again, lost in my imagination and paying little attention to the empirical mess around me. I need to refigure and keep searching. I can return to these musings later. So, on I go. Once I reach the end of a torn up street, I notice what looks like a rather large, perhaps handcrafted archway, with two brass gates dangling precariously from each side. What is left of the dry rock construction is stunning. I enter. All of a sudden the direction of the wind changes and the old stench becomes stronger. I suppose I had gotten somewhat used to this odor over time, but now it strikes me as quite distasteful. It looks like the archway had been attached on both sides to an ancient rock wall and probably at the back as well, so this would have been a large enclosed space. Broken flower pots are in evidence. There seems to be a mix of older and newer buildings. Many must have been colorful as there are a myriad of blue, red, green, and yellow blocks of concrete lying all over, while others were probably plain wood structures. I then discover several small parks within the enclosure; charred grass and bushes and then further a few cracked and crumbling fountains with their exposed and broken water pipes. For some reason, I'm reminded of the fountains somewhat like these in the middle of the city, where I would play in the summer heat when I was young. As I plow through the rubble, I start to find huge bones and what appear to be animal pelts - skins. It strikes me that this must have been an immense museum or group of museums. Back in the day, before everything was digitized, these sorts of attractions were extremely popular. You could see anything from dinosaurs to ants, elephants to spiders, polar bears to penguins, and observe the emergence of evolution and the various branches and limbs extending to primates like me. One of the purposes of these types of places was to preserve a glimpse of the past, so as to have a better understanding of the present. But of course much of this version of the story had changed over time, as more and more information became available and the present rapidly became the future.

When I turn to explore further, I look up and see a strange formation: almost like a blueish - pinkish - redish - orangeish spiral shaped nebula. The materialization of this phenomenon is strikingly beautiful and I'm not sure what to make of it. It seems like there's a stream of luminous purple liquid flowing around inside the spiral with a fixed blue eye at the center, but no face or body. This is an absolutely mind-blowing sight, vision, or whatever it is. I'm stunned. I stand there and stare, in something like a state or trance. Somehow, I sense a presence in this hovering mysterious configuration. I can't tell if it's personal or not. Does it have some communicative capacities other than aesthetic wonders? At this moment, I hear thunder and see lightning, neither of which in my recent experience, if my memory serves me well, has taken place, but there's not a drop of rain. It's almost as if they were a prelude to an important announcement. And sure enough, I then think I hear something like:

> Planet Earth is groaning and weeping. It has been stripped of its resources and left barren. Raging injustice and cosmic corruption, among other travesties, have contributed to this devastation, which took place faster than predicted. Humans brought much of this upon themselves through their woeful lack of care. Millions have died unnecessarily, though a few may have escaped to elsewhere, but life here is close to being over for now.

Astonishing!

I continue to gaze into the gray sky and then perceive the nebula gradually and ever so gently disappears from sight. I sit down for a spell to reflect on this extraordinary encounter. The testimony about the Earth and humanity was familiar and rang true, as well as the possibility that some primates like me, or other forms of beings, escaped elsewhere. The space shuttles that I previously came across could indeed be an indication of this. I'll have to return there to investigate further. But now, I refocus on the museum, which was obviously extremely important for understanding nature and humanity. The natural world was well over a billion – year – old environment, which humans had only recently become part of. Plants and animals and humans were all crucial elements concerning the history of the Earth. Well, to have a history is in some way to have an identity – a people, a nation, an individual and a museum in this context was a marking out, recognizing a trace of something of what it used to be like at certain points in space and time. What it all amounts to, I guess, is a grand story: a mega narrative.

After this short pause delving into the marvels of the past and the present glorious event in the sky, I retrace my steps and head back out of the archway and look for my blue markers. I must have been there longer than I thought because it's getting darker. I should return to the library. Climbing over the debris and other obstacles always seems to take longer on my way back. Yet, I have no way to really tell, so this is just a guess. I now see the last marker I left, so I'm ready to move on from here. When I stop to look for my next marker, I have the strange sensation that someone or something is following me. I've felt this way before, but it was just my imagination running away with me: Nobody and nothing there. Maybe it's the same this time. I find my marker and continue up a desolate street. Darkness is already setting in. The impression of being followed persists, and I want to find out if that's really happening, but I don't want to get off course and lose my way.

Now I'm going to try this to see if anyone or anything is actually following me!

Before darting into an opening in a wall, I make sure I know where my next marker is, and go ahead. I then leap into a huge hole in the ground hidden from view. I narrowly escape a deadly fall into a deeper precipice, regaining my balance just in time on a small ledge. I hope it doesn't give way. After some tense moments, how many I'll never know, an awkward sort of bionic machine creature or whatever it is, comes crashing through the wall, but is unable to stop its momentum and falls into the deep pit and shatters into a hundred pieces before exploding into flames. As I look down into the abyss and see the smoldering metallic carcass, I'm stunned. Not merely because I was actually being followed, but also because I realize how close I was, just a step away, from being down there too. I ponder my own fragility and how life is held by a thread. Then, the fact of being tracked overtakes me. Two questions of many are the first to pop out: Who? and Why? I will have to reflect on these later, as I have to carry on if I'm going to make it back to the library before it's too dark to find the way. Rushing on, but trying to be careful not to get injured, I go from one marker to the next, but each one is harder and harder to see. I start to freak out thinking I'll soon need to find a place to crash for the night. But then I climb up a massive cement block hoping to have just enough light to perceive something. This indeed enables me see a bit better and there in some low lying debris I'm able to locate a marker, and from there find another, and eventually I arrive back at the library with my desk and books.

Phew!

What an eventful sortie. I certainly have some important things to ponder and several new questions to reflect on. They are currently racing around in me. I'm kind of floating in a daze and don't think I'll be able to sleep for a while, although I'm pretty tired. And it's still freezing. I'm hopeful that my cardboard bedding will eventually warm me up. It's a relief to not have to stay somewhere else tonight. So nice to settle into what's familiar. I'm hungry and thirsty. I feel around in the dark until I find my food and water. After eating and drinking, I cover myself up and try to sleep. The events of the day stream before my imaginative eyes like a somewhat blurry film. The tense encounters with palaces, nebula, bionic creatures, and near death, weigh heavily on me and I can't shut them off. Sometimes you don't want to focus or stress about stuff, but it just takes over, especially when trying to sleep. After attempting to count to one hundred and failing, I figure that at last I faded into a shallow, but satisfying sleep.

I awake to murky light and realize that my cardboard covering has again kept me warm enough to sleep through, but it does seem a bit milder today and that feels good. Unfortunately, I fear it will soon be unbearably hot. Like the previous mornings a dream I had comes back to me. I was on a sandy beach surrounded by high cliffs. At first it was night and what looked like millions of stars shone in the pristine sky.

Unfathomable space!

Then two huge space crafts with even brighter lighting came into view. One was gold and red and it faced the other which was black and orange. They fired laser like discharges at each other and after a tremendous clash in the skies, they exploded and fell into the sea. Reminded me of the game palaces and its battle simulations won and lost. I wondered if there were primates like me in these vehicles or was some external power force in charge of the ships' and crews' destiny. It didn't take long to find out. In a matter of minutes hundreds of body parts and digital fragments washed up on the shore. A gruesome, though revealing sight.

Had human primates been interbred with or bred into AI? Had some of them departed planet Earth for other places?

Is this what it all came to? Connect, login! Become an augmented pseudo-human.

If this was the case, whatever your ontological status, some things had not changed. Killing and destruction remained part of the story. I wandered further down the beach, as daylight arrived and looking to my left I saw a cave. I debated with myself about entering. Yes. No. Yes. Finally, I went in. Ten meters from the entrance I noticed intriguing graffiti type writing on the wall. It was faded, but still readable. Beware. Brainwashing tech forces takeover.

CORRUPT.

I'm hunted. Doom. Doom. Doom. I wondered who had taken the trouble to write this and what had happened. At that moment, I turned around, and there were five borg like figures rushing towards me. Chills ran down my spine. I freaked out and woke up. Phew!

These kinds of dreams are scary, but was this really an indication what might be going on here? Had humans or pseudo-humans indeed escaped the devastation and left the Earth? The wedding of technology to humans could have changed their state of being, reducing valuable traits such as empathy or fear and intensifying those of indifference and domination. But what were the forces and powers referred to in the graffiti on the cave wall? This remains an open question that mystifies me.

While getting up, working out, and eating breakfast, one thought continues to haunt me: I was being followed. There had been previous false alarms in this respect, but as far as I could tell, this time it actually happened. Who? and Why? I wonder if whatever it was that fell into the pit was acting on its own accord or if it was taking orders from someone or something else. I lean towards the latter, though there might be other independent agents roaming around serving their own will. But why follow me? Maybe to observe. Maybe to connect. Maybe to capture. There are plenty of other possibilities I suppose, so it's difficult to really come to any conclusions. I can only guess. If I had been able to communicate with my tracker, I would have perhaps found out, though that might have been disturbing if the response was to harm me or to turn me into a machine. Maybe it's better not to know. Well, I figure this is probably about as far as I can take it. I'll just have to wait and see if it happens again.

I need to move on to something else. I think I'll settle at my desk and read. Again, I'm drawn to poetry books and read these lines from another poem by Emily Dickinson, written around 1862.

I measure every Grief I meet
With narrow, probing Eyes –
I wonder if It weighs like Mine –
Or has an Easier size.

I wonder if They bore it Long –
Or did it just begin –
I could not tell the Date of mine –
It feels so old a pain –

I wonder if it hurts to live –
And if They have to try –
And whether – could They choose between –
It would not be – to die –

I note that Some – gone patient long –
At length, renew their smile –
An imitation of a Light –
That has so little Oil –

I wonder if when Years have piled –
Some Thousands – on the Harm –
That hurt them early – such a lapse
Could give them any Balm –

Or would they go on aching still
Through Centuries of Nerve –
Enlightened to a larger Pain –
In Contrast with the Love –

The Grieved – are many – I am told –
There is the various Cause –
Death – is but one – and comes but once –
And only nails the eyes –

There's Grief of Want – and Grief of Cold –
A sort they call "Despair" –
There's Banishment from native Eyes –
In sight of Native Air –

And though I may not guess the kind –
Correctly – yet to me
A piercing Comfort it affords
In passing Calvary –

To note the fashions – of the Cross –
And how they're mostly worn –
Still fascinated to presume
That Some – are like My Own –

Dickinson writes such compelling and heart-felt words. They strike one of the deepest emotions of living in the world: that of Grief. But she also points out that we are not alone. Those valuable traits of fear and empathy are certainly visible here. Her metaphors are lively, even stunning. As I repeat these lines over and over again, I find they have a remarkable rhythm, which spikes imagination and echoes through the memory banks for a long time after reading them.

The experience of grief is indeed common, though diverse, among primates like me and maybe for others too. I don't know. It is, whatever the case, a topic of great significance and much interest. I remember talking this over with family and friends. Grief comes in many different shapes and forms and seems impossible to escape. It has or is going to touch our lives in one way or another. The questions we most discussed were: why and was there any hopeful response? While philosophical, psychological, theological, and ethical perspectives offered some useful insights and were worthwhile studying, it was the poet, poetry, and the poetic that were probably closer to the mark. Poems, metaphors, and stories enhanced imagination and aligned more closely with the feelings and weight of grief. At the end of the day though, the questions ultimately remained:

Who knows why? And is hope a "possible world?"

The enigmas and ambiguities of grief are vastly too complicated and complex to fully understand, yet the "what" of its existence is likely to be recognized by all. I find this poem by Emily Dickinson so striking I read it over and over again. Somehow simple, yet profound; it touches deeply – right down to the bones and marrow. I'll keep it with me as I go on.

Even though it's getting hotter, I should venture out of the library to pursue my investigations. Maybe I'll re-visit some of the locations that were more promising in offering clues, but then again if I go into a new region I may strike gold. After going back and forth between the options, I finally decide to go for gold. I take some orange markers along and start off. This new direction isn't any easier than the others. There are piles of debris and rubbish all over and the stench seems stronger. Winding my way through the ruins I notice more charred grass, bushes, and felled trees. Looks like this may have once been a gorgeous boulevard. I carry on for quite a distance and I then turn right and pass through several corridors that eventually bring me into a large square. The gray and brown buildings here, now partially standing, must have once been huge. They're still pretty high in spite of roofs being torn off and part of the walls broken down. I wonder if they might be worth exploring or should I move on. I think about this for a spell and then decide to take a closer look. I enter the shell of a structure with its massive doors and beveled windows blown out. Need to be careful as everything seems unstable; something could fall at any moment, even without an earthquake: This thought makes me shudder. I remember all too well the last time that happened. Totally freaked me. Moving slowly through the remains, I notice that I'm walking on something hyper solid. I stamp my foot down and there's no give at all. That's unusual. As I go on it seems that this is the case for the entire ground floor. So, this is gigantic and covers the length and width of the whole place. Maybe it's just one big block of concrete. Then I see a large plaque lying in the rubble. From what I can make out after reading the inscription, it appears that this was some kind of government building. Perhaps, all the buildings in the square were in some way connected to each other. Further exploration may give me a clue about this, but for the moment I want to focus on what's underneath me. There's no way I can remove all the wreckage from the top to locate any openings up here, but once I climb down and walk around the exterior of the building I get a better perspective. It slowly becomes clear that this huge 'thing' is probably some kind of underground steel bunker. Government building and steel bunker spike imagination and curiosity. I want to find out what's in there, but at the same time I'm a bit hesitant and uncertain about what I might discover. When I reach the end of the bunker on the west side, I notice a small door with a big lever on it – could be some kind of emergency entry/exit. I stop and reflect on whether I should try to get in, or just go on to what's next. I hesitate. I'm not sure. After some time, who knows how long, my curiosity outweighs my reluctance. I attempt to move the lever from one side to the other, but to no avail. Maybe it's not a door after all. I need something solid to force the lever over. I find a medium sized rock. That might do. I hold the stone with my two hands and push on the lever, and it pops to the other side. I'm able to pull on the door and crawl through into the bunker. My eyes have to adjust. I can see that the light here is coming in via a few small portholes. The first thing I notice is there are masses of robots scattered around. Looks as if they were hard at work doing something, but are now frozen in space and time. For how long? What happened?

Who knows?

Moving around these inoperative robots and in the direction of a vast room at the center of the bunker, I see there is an enormous panel with maybe a hundred screens. An intact and somewhat luxurious chair sits in front of the panel with its back to me, but out of the blue it suddenly spins around. Sitting in it is this emaciated horrific looking creature or construction. Alive or dead?

It is covered with a pale animal type skin with veins that seem to be flowing with blood. A black hooded robe hangs off its frame/body and I see sharp white eyes with no pupils. Phew! Freaky. I'm in a state of shock and have trouble catching my breath.

What is this?

As the ghastly thing gets up and comes towards me, my hands start to tremble.

What's going on?

But just as it reaches me it collapses to the ground and disintegrates – gone. I actually had no idea whether this hooded character meant me any harm or was trying to tell me something of value for the present and future. I wonder what that was all about. I feel a strange mixture of uncertainty, fear, and sadness; strong emotions surge through me. After the rush of sensations subsides a bit, I continue to search through the bunker. Rifling through drawers and cabinets doesn't produce much and I figure I better be on my way. I crawl back out through the bunker door and I'm hit by the excruciating heat. Scorching, even though it is overcast and gray.

I forge on through the rubble to what appears to be the next building in the square. On one partially standing wall there are some only slightly damaged photos; images of primates like me in precarious, even desperate circumstances, including war, poverty, and famine. There's a tattered banner underneath that says: relief and restore. I'd wager this probably was a humanitarian aid organization. Next to the photos is what looks like a message board enclosure, which is smashed, but amazingly I find a few pages in the debris that are still somewhat readable. However, the information on them is dire. Pandemics swept the Earth killing millions. They were almost unstoppable. This reminds me of the awful dream I had earlier. In addition to this, famine ravaged many regions of the world and millions died of starvation. Lastly, the climate had become so chaotic and unpredictable that not only food resources and water were scarce, but infrastructures collapsed bringing an end to transportation and distribution. Due to these dire circumstances all humanitarian efforts ceased. I'm stunned and have to sit down on a block of concrete, my head pounding with these catastrophic accounts. While some of this is not entirely new to me, the magnitude of it is shocking.

How could humanity have let such a thing happen?

When the status quo of the unsustainable is embraced for profit and the conditions for healthy life on planet Earth ignored, I'd wager the outcome would be this. So many suffered and died. What a calamity! This is deeply troubling, yet the accounts of these devastating results do give me a few clues, and slight glimpse into something of what's going on here and why I find myself alone, but there must be more. After reflecting on these things, for how long I'll never know, I move off with a heavy heart to explore other parts of the square.

The rubble is piled up pretty high in some places, so I rummage through what appears to be a couple of flattened out buildings, but don't find anything of interest. On the south side of the square I come upon hundreds of satellite antennas lying on the ground. There was probably a global telecommunications office around here somewhere. Just next to them I notice some marble steps and next to them there are twenty or so huge built-in generators, most likely installed to protect against power shortages or black-outs. They're intact, but completely dead. It would be fascinating to find out who was connecting to whom in what appears to have been a vast and complex network of sophisticated interactions. I keep searching through the debris around this site and eventually uncover several steel tubes about two meters long and ten centimeters wide. They seem to have been protected from serious damage, but why they're here is an open question. Before looking at these more carefully, I also notice lying around in the vicinity there are some smashed telescope pieces, broken GPS systems, and shattered measuring equipment, once all pretty powerful and sophisticated looking technology.

But for what?

Then, I open the tubes. This takes some work, but I manage. Inside each tube I find a large rolled up sheet of sturdy paper covered with complex diagrams, but it's hard to get a good idea of what's here. I need ten hands and feet to unroll them all and keep them flat. I carry the papers to a wide area, unroll them one at a time, putting debris on the four corners of each paper, so I can now look at them all at once, and hopefully make sense of them. After close study, I begin to wonder if these sheets are possibly some kind of blueprints. There are graphs, maps, charts, tables, and what appear to be travel trajectories and construction sites. No names or destinations are mentioned, but it looks as if they're referring to outer space and the galactic, not Earth. Considering the antennas, generators, other technical paraphernalia, and now these scrolls of multifaceted information, I'd wager this may have been a world-wide center for monitoring older space stations and planning the locations of new ones. If this was the case, they were massive in scope from what I can tell (something akin to a big city of thousands or even millions of inhabitants). And the future construction platforms appeared to be even more gigantic. So, were these drafts related to a great migration - an exodus of unimaginable proportions? And if so, why were they left behind? Was someone or something planning to come back for them? From all the data it appears that an evacuation process could have been a well-planned out endeavor aiming to give every possible chance of moving to another environment and surviving there, after the awful failure on planet Earth. Though this seems a likely possibility and a partial indication of why no one is around but me, I'm left with a myriad of questions to reflect on. Was there really a magnificent departure of some sort? If so, who or what was behind it? Did they leave on their own or were they forced? What were the travel numbers like? Where was the destination? Did anyone actually make it? These remain unanswered queries for the moment, but the results of my tedious search today are very intriguing.

At this point, darkness is beginning to hover over me and I figure I should make my way back to the library. Before leaving, I ponder what to do with the sheets of information. No use in taking them with me, so I roll up the blueprints, put them back in the tubes and lay them close to where I found them. It will be easy enough to locate them again if I need to, or if anyone or anything returns for them they will be close to where I first saw them. I think back to the huge space shuttle factories that I visited previously and imagine that there may very well be a connection between these two locations. I'll have to check it out and revisit the massive industrial complexes soon to see if I may have missed something on my previous expedition. Looking around the square, I now see one of my orange markers and start off in the direction I came from.

On the way, I pass what are likely to be the remains of a digital mega store. There are thousands of computers, devices, and phones strewn around a large area. And all at once I'm reminded of a mobile phone call I had with a friend before my present state came over me. We had a long chat that went in many directions. From tolerance to intolerance, ecology to pollution, justice to mercy, life to death. These and many other topics we discussed were significant, but I vividly recall talking about the complex issue of narrative within history and fiction? Should we assume that historical and fictional literature are clearly different? Are works of history "true" in a way that fictional literary works are not? This field of inquiry is so vast that we could hardly cover it in one phone call. We nevertheless brought up the question if narratives should be read as "historicized fiction" or "fictionalized history," or in some other fashion all together. There are always more questions than answers, so that's about as far as it went, but the conversation and the issues that were raised then stayed with me. While reminiscing about the phone call, I suddenly have a flash back to the museum I recently came across and I remember some of the relics from what was once suggested to be history. Well, then, I ask myself again: what is or was history?

Moving back into the present from the marvel of being able to imaginatively remember notions of the past, I turn to the west and see another orange marker, which enables me to continue on my way.

Progress is slow as I have to take a number of detours to avoid high mounds of rubble. On one of these occasions, I come across what looks like pools of blood, but no flesh or bones are around. I wonder if all this jelled blood like substance is animal or human. Could the flesh and bones have been "harvested" and used for something else? What a gruesome question, for which of course, at the moment, I have no answer. After pondering this for a spell, how long I'll never know, I need to concentrate and focus on finding the next orange marker. I look around, but can't see it. Heading cautiously on in the same direction, not wanting to go too far for fear of getting lost, I find before long much to my relief another marker. So far, so good. But my relief is short lived as I notice the gloomy gray sky darkening. Visibility is rapidly decreasing and I'm getting paranoid that I won't find my way back to the library in time. I try to pick up the pace, but I remain somewhat bothered by the cumbersome terrain. It's really tough to be patient in these circumstances, but I don't have much choice about things like this in the world which I live. Well, that profound yet unanswerable question strikes me again - how much choice do humans ever really have?

Who knows?

For some reason, I gaze into the heavens and something there catches my eye. One by one red letters appear in the dark gray sky and suddenly there floats the word *light*. At the same moment, a beam like ray, shines down upon me. It's almost as if this is a stage light that moves with me wherever I go. Its origin escapes me. I can't see past the thick blustery clouds or the lettering to detect the source of light, but for now it's a welcome illumination. I don't try to figure this one just yet and go with the flow. I still have to locate my markers to get back home. In due time, I find one and then eventually others, and I'm guided back to the library.

When I arrive the light goes out and the red letters disappear. This is weird. Unexplainable! It's great to be here, but I'm so tired. All I can do is eat and sleep. Even though the heat is stifling, which usually means I have a difficult time falling asleep, this time I must have gone out pretty quickly since I don't remember much tossing or turning.

When I awake in the morning it's still sweltering. I need a break from this intense heat, but also dread the thought of the piercing cold returning. Such unmanageable extremes are frustrating and debilitating, and though it had been attempted by many previously, weather control is beyond my reach. I just sit there and after a few minutes, imaginative memory chimes in and a bizarre dream from last night comes back to me.

I was wandering in the rubble pondering my fate and the state of my surroundings when some kind of phenomenon (creature/being?) appeared, as it were in the heavenlies. It was dressed in a hooded maroon robe with a multi-colored belt, but had no eyes, nose, mouth, or hands. Below the hood, in place of the face, was a large question mark, sort of like stuck on a screen. I just stood staring. I wondered if this was a programed hallucination. Just then the display or whatever it was started to blink as if someone had pushed the start button. As I focused on the flickering question mark, it became almost hypnotic, but all of a sudden the red letters of *light* appeared, and after some time, I'll never know how long, a beaming ray shone down from the densely clouded dark sky. Then it all vanished.

My dream seems to echo in some way what I experienced the previous day, but there are few insights in it to actually help me interpret what occurred then. While this robed character could have been the source of light, there was no explanatory information as to who this was, why it happened, or if I was to understand something more from it than the experience itself. Sometimes stuff just happens, but perhaps I'm missing a sign, a meaning, a message revealed in the dream. I madly attempt to dredge deeper into the tremendous, though bizarre, marvel of human memory, but nothing else rises to the surface. I reflect more on the dream. Could this unusual character with a question mark instead of a face have come to me both in a conscious and dream state? At any rate, it didn't do me any harm in either one, and actually had been helpful illuminating my way back to the library. I guess it's still an enigma, and I wonder whether the flashing question mark is some kind of confirmation of what I'm left with: few answers and lots of questions. This may seem perfectly normal for someone in my situation, yet it's also extremely difficult to accept, since my natural tendency is geared toward understanding: discover, elucidate, clarify, what it all means.

Life is strange. Seems to me humans are made up of weird physical and mental complexities. They have remarkable abilities, yet significant weaknesses. Their sophisticated, yet under-utilized brains seem to be both a blessing and a curse. New frontiers in engineered evolution were out to enhance its capacities and eventually get rid of all the flaws for survival; robots, borgs, and pseudo-humans became the fittest survivors – but to live into the future you had to plug in. Connect or die. Given the option what would I decide? Connect and live another life in a different environment somewhere out in space, or remain on planet Earth and eventually cease to exist. Would the gain of one be better than the loss of the other? I feel like I'm coming apart at the seams in my present circumstances, but I realize that any human would probably feel this way, and that the challenge I face now is still something I want to turn into, rather than moving away from.

I take a break from these meandering, yet significant thoughts and get up to do a few exercises. It's so hot and I'm already sweating before doing anything. After a short workout, I eat and drink something. My energy levels seem low, so I eat more than usual hoping to feel stronger. Dealing with the extreme heat and the continual dreary gray sky is exhausting and oppressing, so I decide to return to my desk and read some more poetry. I look through a few options and then decide to return to Wordsworth; I always am challenged and captivated by his insightful words.

Memory

A pen – to register; a key –
That winds through secret wards;
Are well assigned to Memory
By allegoric Bards.

As aptly, also, might be given
A pencil to her hand;
That, softening objects, sometimes even
Outstrips the heart's demand:
That smooths foregone distress, the lines
Of lingering care subdues,
Long-vanished happiness refines,
And clothes in brighter hues;

Yet like a tool of Fancy, works
Those Spectres to dilate
That startle Conscience, as she lurks
Within her lonely seat.

O! that our lives, which flie so fast,
In purity were such,
That not an image of the past
Should fear that pencil's touch!

Retirement then might hourly look
Upon a soothing scene,
Age steal to his allotted nook
Contented and serene;

With heart as calm as lakes that sleep,
In frosty moonlight glistening;
Or mountain rivers, where they creep
Along a channel smooth and deep,
        To their own far-off murmurs listening.

This is such an astonishing poem. I can't help but read it over again several times. Wordsworth's words ignite profound longings and reflections. Memory is indeed an elusive and a fascinating dimension of being human. Something like a vast vault, only partially decrypted through writing, and only to some extent unlocked by metaphorical keys, but also filled with hazy scenes, fragmented pieces of past relationships, experiences, thoughts, dreams, victories and defeats, joys and sorrows. Who could figure out memory? Its shadowy, yet visceral character is a remarkable mystery.

While still reflecting on the splendor of this poem and the complexities of memory, I turn to read a few more lines from another illuminating poem by Wordsworth: *The Prelude*, Book 13.

Meanwhile, the Moon look'd down upon this shew
In single glory, and we stood, the mist
Touching our very feet; and from the shore
At a distance not the third part of a mile
Was a blue chasm; a fracture in the vapour,
A deep and gloomy breathing-place through which
Mounted the roar of waters, torrents, streams
Innumerable, roaring with one voice.

These spiking imagination metaphors anchored in nature give rise to thought. There is both a stark beauty and haunting power portrayed in this part of the poem. I can somehow see myself standing in the mist, viewing the chasm, and hearing the growling sounds, as if I'm part of the scene, so graphically written by the poet.

Forged by Wordsworth and his poetic art, I'm now ready to leave the library and continue my explorations. After previously discovering the tubes containing the plans for what looked like space travel and the construction of massive space cities, I want to go back to the remains of the industrial complex Mars XXX to see if I can find any more information. I'll follow my gray markers left from last time and hope they are all still in place to guide the way. As I start out, I see a couple, but after a while I become a bit leery that I'm heading in the right direction. It's difficult to know whether to continue on in the same track or to veer off one way or the other in hopes of locating more markers. My decision making processes are not improving and after a brief rest to think this over I decide to move cautiously forward in the same direction. After some time, how long I'll never know, I spot another gray marker. Phew! I'm grateful that I didn't bail out and change directions too soon. So, I'm still on the right path.

Trudging through the debris seems to be getting tougher and tougher, or maybe my capacity to keep up with it is diminishing. I'm really not sure, but this feels like harder and harder work. Climbing over the piled up concrete blocks and other wreckage, especially in the densely built-up areas, is an out-and-out challenge. After going on for a spell, I see a partially standing grayish/blackish brick wall, say about four meters high and four wide, and at its bottom there is a one meter oval shaped opening. I didn't notice this the first time I passed here, but maybe it just emerged recently. Things tend to appear and disappear all the time. I'm curious about this opening and where it might lead, but I need to be cautious and reflect carefully on any detours at this point. Figuring I can take a quick look and then carry on to my destination, I finally, after how long I'll never know, decide to check it out. I hesitate and reassess my decision, and though inner tension is high, I go ahead. Curiosity wins.

As I step through the opening, it first appears to be illuminated, but quickly becomes dark. This freaks me out. I turn around, to go out, but am utterly taken back by what I now face. There blocking my way is a massive gruesome looking machine or creature with one purple eye gleaming through grill marks or bars in lieu of a face. No ears, or mouth that I can see, but two short antennae stem from what is probably a stainless steel head covering. That's all I have time to capture. In shock, I step backwards, and lose my balance falling through the opening, and sliding into and then down a long tube type structure, somehow preserved from damage. When I get to the bottom or wherever I am, it's cold and damp. There are slivers of light shining through the debris and reflecting off shattered glass. As my eyes adjust to the relative obscurity, I see knights in white fleece and shiny silver plated armor holding laser beamers and standing at attention as if ready for battle. But I soon realize there are no knights. Empty armor is all that's left. Nobody there. They appear to be lifeless disconnected machines from what I can tell.

Even though at the moment I don't feel threatened by these unanimated knights, my inclination is to get out of this enclosure or whatever it is, yet I hesitate to go back the way I came in. It's steep and slippery, and I worry that the machine or creature is still waiting for me at the opening. Maybe I can find another exit, but what awaits me down here is an unknown. I guardedly take a few steps forward into the cavern. I then turn right and creep down a lengthy jagged corridor. Halfway, I suddenly feel a tremor and a jolt, and quickly realize this is another earthquake. Now I'm totally freaking out. This location is so much worse than being out in the open, which is already bad enough. I'm really not sure what to do, keep going, turn back, stay put. My mind is blown, but I must try to stay calm and find shelter. I don't see anything that looks like a safe place. Things continue to shake and I become even more alarmed as suddenly about ten meters in front of me, huge cement blocks collapse down into this apparent underground fortress. I hit the ground and don't move at all, but I fear what is coming. I'll soon be crushed – buried alive. Eventually things stop moving, and what's right above me has not yet caved in. Phew!

After the dust and debris settle some, I wipe the dirt off my face and then notice streaks of light piercing through the avalanche up ahead. I carefully crawl towards them and see that the earthquake, as it turns out, has created small openings between the concrete blocks. To try and escape through one of these is risky, but I might just make it. I scramble up the blocks towards one of the small openings and then attempt to squeeze through it. But to no avail. It's a tiny crack and I can't make it, so I have to come back down and look for a bigger one without causing the whole pile to cave in even further. I explore a couple of other potential exit cracks, but don't get far. I reckon I may not get out of here. At this point, I really freak out. But then I look down, and notice at the bottom of the concrete blocks a space that looks big enough for me to actually crawl through. This looks promising, but I can't really see far, so I have no idea where I'm going to end up. I get down on my stomach and squeeze inside the opening. Crawling forward I start to get paranoid about possibly getting stuck. In my haste, I didn't think this through carefully enough before diving in. I can't stand up or turn around to go back. The sole option is to keep on going. My arms, stomach, and legs sting, so I must be pretty scratched up. I turn a corner once to the right then to the left, and I'm relieved to see a glimmer of light roughly twenty-five meters ahead. When I finally reach it I see this is clearly an opening, but I still wonder if it will be big enough for me to squeeze through and slip outside. I think I can just get my shoulders in and if I can angle them in the right direction my whole body should be able to follow. So I pull myself up and slowly slither through, my hands and feet barely cooperating, but finally I escape.

Phew! Wow!

That was close and I'm very grateful to have made it out, even without being able to explore any further. It's a hyper relief to be free from that claustrophobic enclosure. Sometimes to be curious is beneficial, sometimes it isn't. I take a look at my cuts and scrapes, which seem to be superficial, and likely heal fairly quickly.

After resting some, how long I'll never know, I get back on track to where I was headed before my curiosity lured me into what became a near death trap. I quickly notice that it is cooler, which is welcome, but I wager that it will soon be freezing, which is not. Searching around for my gray markers may be even more complicated after the post-earthquake re-distribution of some of the wreckage. It appears I'm not so far from where I entered the hole in the wall, so I'm able to somewhat get my bearings, but I'm not sure which direction from here is the right one. The cloud cover is heavier today; billowing white and silver masses interlaced with blackish wisps, and as usual this scenario makes it difficult to discern what's ahead. I take several steps over the debris and then jump from one concrete block to another for a while, and lo and behold, I find another marker. From this point, I keep my line and easily locate marker after marker until I find myself in the area of the immense industrial complexes I had previously visited.

Once at the Mars XXX locations I once again re-imagine what these ruined buildings would have looked like: magnificent structures incorporating a monumental array of ingenious capacities for production. Visualizing this scene is like falling into a material, yet imaginary world that goes far beyond my sensory experience. Could some form of primates like me have launched into space from here and now be living somewhere else? Was this a viable option? Had the reality that life on planet Earth was no longer sustainable pushed the creative and technological tool kits of our huge brains to their momentarily ultimate potential? Maybe. I still find the whole scenario rather crazy, but the detailed plans I had seen earlier in the tubes and the previous discoveries I made here all seem to point in the direction that a space escape was indeed a reasonable possibility.

Who knows? Maybe someone or something does, but not me.

At any rate, this time I have to look at things more carefully. Whatever I can find out might help to confirm or negate an exodus into space. When I enter the hanger of Mars XXX, it seems familiar and I recognize much of what I see before me, but I have to keep a sharp eye out for something new. The big picture here seems clear enough, but I'm looking for more specific details. I start plowing through the debris, some of which is too heavy to lift up and look under. I'm overwhelmed and not sure I can get any more information out of this mess, but I figure it's worth a try. I wish there was a way to reconstruct these fragments via a simulation process or some neuro faculty that would take me back in time. Of course, this is beyond my abilities, and imagination is about as close as I can come to its realization. Imagination can be, but not always is, an accurate "informer," so as I go on, I have to weigh up other viable possibilities that may emerge from the wreckage. Rummaging closer and closer to the gigantic transporter leads me to an area where there are smaller pieces of rubble. I sit down on the remains of a dilapidated chair to examine them, then kick away layers of soft debris nearby.

For some mysterious reason, I drift into reflecting on the emergence and disappearance of life forms on the planet. What a fascinating topic to ponder, but I realize I have very little knowledge or information concerning these big arcs in time and space. Who knows how it really all began and came to an end? The immemorial – deep time escapes me, but so, to a significant extent does my current context. Perhaps, someone who is infinite would know it all. And maybe that was the great longing of much of humanity – to know – to know definitively what's behind the screen of time and space. I must have lapsed into a sort of daydream thinking about these things because all of a sudden I'm jarred out of my reverie and find myself on the ground next to the chair. I guess I just tipped over.

From this low lying perspective, I'm able to scan around at ground level and I eventually see what appears to be a slightly raised shard of metal or corner piece of steel protruding from the rubble, which I might not have detected had I not fallen off the chair. I scramble over several obstacles to get a closer look. It appears to be some kind of small safe or vault. I retrieve an iron bar and attempt to clear away the clutter that has built up around it. Once this is done, I use the bar to pry the encased vault out of the ground. It looks like it only has three sides as the fourth side, perhaps the door, has been ripped off by some forceful impact. There is lots of dirt inside, but when I feel around my fingers touch something like a piece of hard plastic and I take it out. After wiping it off, I see it's a digital code pass. I wonder what this is for. I quickly look around for something to unlock, not that this pass will work without energy, but maybe I can somehow get in to whatever it was used for. I search around beneath the transporter, but come up empty. There's nothing that a digital code pass could open. I backup about nine or ten meters and carefully look over the mass of wreckage again. This new vantage point gives me a better perspective and the shape of a huge cabinet emerges from under a pile of debris. It will take a while to clear the rubble from the area, but this seems promising, so I'll go for it. When I finish, after how long I'll never know, I discover that it is indeed an enormous cabinet and that fortunately it is lying face up. I don't see any place on the doors to put in the pass, and I'm perplexed. Not that it really matters since the pass won't work anyway, but it would have been nice to know if that was indeed its function. After clearing away more debris, I notice on the top side there is a slot. I try the pass and sure enough it fits. This is pretty good confirmation that there may be high level security information stored in here. But how to get in? I hunt around for a thin, but strong blade like instrument to slide between the massive doors and try to force one open. There's so much junk lying around it shouldn't be a problem to find something. A few meters away I pick up a piece that just might work, but after a few attempts I realize that while solid enough, it is too thick. I head off in another direction and find a few other things to try.

When I get back to the cabinet I think to myself this is never going to work, nevertheless I have to keep at it. Several instruments fail to do anything, but then I'm able to get a hefty piece of steel into the small space between the doors, however, I can't get enough leverage, so they don't budge. I need another one or maybe two more pieces like this. As I turn to search for something similar, I hear an eerie creaking sound. My first thought is another earthquake, yet this is quickly dismissed, since the ground is not moving. It seems like the noise is coming from above me somewhere. Then I notice that one of the pylons still holding up the massive transporter is wobbling and the friction is causing a sort of screeching sound. If this thing goes down it will be big trouble. I'll be buried alive under loads of debris. I start running to try and get as far as I can from the launch site. When I think I've gone far enough to be out of danger, I sit down and watch. The pylon, all of a sudden, lurches to the right and I hide my eyes, but hearing no crash I look up and see it did not give way entirely. It seems to have settled for the moment and is still holding the transporter up from a total collapse. Though, who knows for how long? The unnerving noise stops and it's silent again. I'm desperate to go back over to the cabinet, but I must first find a couple more steel type blades to maybe get it open. Scrounging, yet again, through more rubble I finally find two pieces that look right and

I also take with me two bigger rods that might help open the doors, once I hopefully get the smaller ones in place. So, now I cautiously return towards the cabinet. I have been so preoccupied and gone through so many ups and downs, I haven't noticed until now that it is getting dark. This freaks me out and stops me in my tracks. The possibility that I'll have to stay somewhere other than the library sends chills down my spine. I have to re-focus my energy and decide what to do. Stay put or rush back?

The light is fast dwindling and a dense obscurity is closing in. I don't reckon I can get to the library in time, so I resign myself to being stuck out here for the night.

Leaving my tools there I quickly move as far away from the transporter as possible and start looking for some place suitable to sleep. This is tough to find since there's so much debris and rubble all over. I'd like to feel protected, yet I fear getting under anything that might suddenly collapse. Eventually, I come upon what must have been used to cover seats in the transporter. I clear a space on the buckled floor and spread the material out. This will have to do. I don't need much of a cover and only some padding. It's now completely dark, so I should try to sleep. I'm pretty agitated, but hope I can doze off and will only wake when it's lighter. Thoughts and questions continue to swirl around in my imaginative musings and I try to block these out by counting, though at first without much success. Sleep, oh more precious than gold, silver, or diamonds. Sleep, so vital for the human body and brain. I'd wager there are not many things for me more frustrating than not being able to sleep.

Somewhere around two hundred and forty, as far as I can remember, I fall asleep, because after I wake up. Darkness is still everywhere. How long, I wonder, before the first few glimmers of light?

I lie, still flat on my back, and then remember a vivid dream I probably just had. I was here, in this very dilapidated industrial complex and I was asleep. My eyes gradually opened and I took a peek. No light. I felt oppressive heat weighing down on me. So hot. I wasn't really sure what to do next, but after a spell I leaned up on my elbow and looked around. Hard to make much out, to my left – mounds, lumpy shapes, objects hanging from the caved in roof. I slowly turned to my right and thought I saw something like human beings seated in the transporter, as if waiting to take off. I scrambled to my feet and headed off in that direction. I tripped over debris several times and banged up my knee, but kept going. As I got closer, I saw the masses on board the transporter were looking towards me. But in a weird sort of way they appeared vacant, almost unreal. I wondered why. Had they been transformed in some way? A fusing of the brain with an artificially intelligent stimulator that re-engineered the complete nature of being a human, perhaps thus making it possible to enter outer space and stay there? I had no idea. A dream minute or two later, the transporter door closed and it took off disappearing through the clouds.

This vivid imagery is probably what startled me out of dream mode and back to wake mode. As I lie here trying to decrypt this dream, I know it's very unlikely that I'll be able to get back to sleep. I wonder, if I had been given the option presented in my dream, would I have left the Earth? Would any survival context be better than none? This difficulty of a choice with all its ambiguities and possibilities, keeps spinning around in my imagination as I desperately wait for it to get lighter, and ever so gradually, or so it seems, it does.

After the murky light finally arrives, I'm still wrestling with my dream. Did humans, and perhaps pseudo-humans, really escape the catastrophic and toxic environment of Earth in transporters to live somewhere in space? How trustworthy are dreams as an "informer?" When I get up, I notice blood on my pants and feel a bruise somewhere around the knee area. Wait a minute, I remember banging up a knee in my dream and now it appears to have really happened. Usually, the dream state is somewhat distinct from the awake state, but here there seems to be a bewildering level of symmetry between the two. So cryptic!

How could this be?

Perhaps, my memory is starting to fail me. Or maybe in some contexts states of consciousness are beginning to ebb and flow, merge and demerge, as it were. Something's happening here and I don't know what it is.... something I've never experienced before. I'm completely baffled by this phenomenon, and it surely goes far beyond my limited understanding of memory, consciousness, dreams, and their relation or lack of it, to human life. I won't be able to let this event go and will probably reflect on it a lot more, but I'm not likely to figure it out anytime soon, so I better move on.

I need to get back to the cabinet and try again to open it. Retrieving my thin steel type blades and heftier rods, I'm ready to go to work. But while making my way over towards the cabinet, something incredible takes place. When I step around a pile of debris, I happen to put my foot on a metal plaque and it reacts something like a pedal. As it goes down a few centimeters, I hear the cabinet doors unlock. It's like a Zing, or whatever. I'll take it. I go over and try to pull open one heavy door and then the other, but they won't open more than a few centimeters. I wonder if this is a mechanism of some kind or because the doors are so heavy, since the cabinet is lying flat on its back. Maybe I need to prop them up with something strong so they stay fully open. But I think of an even better option. If I can find some rope and tie the doors to a solid footing, maybe that will work. It's worth a try, so I head off in search of rope. Rambling around in all this mess is arduous, but there must be some rope around here somewhere. All of a sudden, it dawns on me that I could use electrical cable or wiring to the same effect. There's plenty of that strewn about. Finding a sharp edged metal bracket nearby, I proceed to cut several two meter long pieces. Once this is done, I head back over towards the cabinet. On my way, I realize that blood from my knee is now running down my leg and I feel exhaustion starting to overwhelm me. I'm hungry and thirsty and need to patch up my wound, but curiosity and imagination of possibilities compel me to carry on. Arriving at the cabinet, I again step on the pedal and the doors pop open slightly. I quickly tie some wiring around the handle and then use a heavy piece of metal in the ground as a type of winch and gradually pull open the door and secure it with a knot. For the moment it holds, so I do the same with the other door. Now the cabinet is wide open, but to my utter amazement it appears to be empty. This is highly disillusioning. I was anticipating more clues. I'm deeply discouraged and stare at the void before me. I keep gazing into the vacant space, then slowly move back. My eyes go from top to bottom and I still don't see anything. After a spell, how long I'll never know, I once again move closer and notice that the shelves are pretty thick. A spark of hope rushes through me. Maybe there's something hidden in them. My heartbeat increases and my energy surges. It takes some patience to figure out how to open the shelves, but when I finally do succeed I find a number of documents; graphs, plans, sheets of calculations, drawings and so forth. Astonishingly, these look very similar to what I previously found in the tubes.

Wow! Double Wow!

This is incredible.

As I look through them I seem to have for the first time a partial confirmation of a space escape. From the combined evidence, it now seems highly probable that some kind of international evacuation effort had been undertaken to get anyone still alive on the Earth into space. Survival beckoned. There were probably thousands of these launching sites located strategically across the globe. This is an exhilarating discovery for me. I'm totally elated. I wonder how many escaped. Where did they go? Space stations, space cities? And did they survive? If so, what kind of life do they have now? But I still wonder 'why' this scenario was necessary? What happened here to require such a radical solution? All these unanswerable questions surface, at least for the time being, but I can always imagine a myriad of possibilities.

It's time to clean up my bloody knee and then get back to the library for something to eat, drink, and read. After looking more closely at my injury I see it's not too bad, so I'll wait until I have access to some water to wash it before bandaging it up if necessary. Now to find my way home. In the midst of these collapsed Mars XXX complexes and the world they contain, I need to locate my first gray marker so I can start off in the right direction into another world. I notice it's getting even cooler, as the extreme weather swings continue. The freezing cold is on its way again, or so it seems, unless something changes. This makes it all the more important for me to get to my shelter as quickly as possible. Unfortunately, the dense fog that is now billowing around complicates matters, and it's even more arduous than usual, yet from time to time it opens up and I'm able to see more clearly.

From here there are plenty of different directions to go. I start out to my right trudging over considerable amounts of wreckage, but after carefully searching, I don't find anything. The initial marker eludes me. I move off to the left rambling through the debris, but no luck on this side either. It must be somewhere in this vicinity. I decide, after some reflection, that I should widen the range of my search further away from the launch site and cabinet. When I do, and the fog clears some, I eventually discover one and then in looking ahead see another, so I'm on my way. Yet, climbing over a high pile of rubble leaves me in a precarious situation. I'm facing an arduous decent. When I carefully start down the other side the bricks and mortar are treacherous and I slip. My legs are up in the air and I'm flat on my back in no time. Happens so quickly it blows my mind. I struggle to get up and feel some pain in my hips and knees, but nothing compared to the pain in my left hand and in particular my thumb.

As I look down I realize why!

My thumb is at a weird angle, broken or dislocated. Ouch. Only one way to fix this. I pull hard on it and the dislocated joint pops back into place, though not without pain. Phew! Not broken. It feels better now, but I won't be able to use it much for a while. My hand is trembling and starting to swell and I feel a bit disoriented. I quickly remove the rings from my left hand and put them on my right, which already has quite a few. After some time, who knows how long, I hit the road again so to speak and continue my journey back to the library. The fog has now dissipated. As I ramble on from one marker to the next, I make good progress until I'm side tracked by a lively looking banshee with a yellow and purple wand. I seem to be getting somewhat used to these strange encounters. This being like character is dressed in a flowing red costume with a shiny black top hat and a wild pair of giant green shoes. It is gesturing for me to take a detour around a colossal hole in the ground. I probably would have done this anyway, so what's the point? Not sure what to make of this and the familiar notions of suspicion and trust immediately kick in.

Where did this apparition come from?
Who does it represent, if anyone?
Is it out to harm me? To trick me?
Should I accept its signals?
I suppose. Well, I'm not sure.

Wait.

Now it's motioning me with the wand to come over to where it's standing. I notice it seems to be fascinated by the rings on my right hand. I'd rather keep going and avoid any potential difficulties here, but every step I take is matched, and it doesn't look like I can escape without further engagement of some kind. Reluctantly, I move in a bit closer, and I take off two of my rings and hold them out. The banshee tilts its head as if trying to understand what I'm doing. My aim is to offer these as a gift and with a little prodding, extending the rings again and again, it eventually reaches out and takes them; my gift is accepted. At the same moment, this mystifying character touches my thumb with its wand and my pain and swelling are immediately gone. In the next instant, the banshee vanishes, but curiously the wand is left behind dangling in mid-air. I go to grab it, but it disintegrates into the rest of the rubble on the ground. This whole sequence of events is astonishing and I have much to reflect on, but for now I must get around the massive crater. Continue! After some considerable effort, I finally locate another marker on the other side and I'm heading in the right direction again. My energy levels are dropping substantially and the freezing cold is getting harder and harder to fight. Darkness is almost upon me, so pushing on remains essential. Unfortunately, I can't go too fast. It's slippery and I can't risk falling again. Better to keep a steady pace and the best footing possible. Eventually, I find one marker after another and now I can see that I'm almost there. What an immense relief! One hundred meters or so and I'll be home.

After I warm up a little and I settle back into the library, I eat, drink, and rest. I then attend to my knee. Fortunately, I don't need a bandage. Nothing too serious. This brings me back to the remarkable encounter with the banshee who accepted my rings and healed my thumb, which was a pretty severe injury. I just can't help but shake my head as I imaginatively re-visit this phenomenal experience. Pretty amazing and frankly all together baffling to reflect on – in an eerie kind of way, almost dream like. Nevertheless, what I do know is that my rings were accepted as a gift and that my thumb was healed, so I'd wager something really good happened through this wild meeting. The configuration of the scenario, however, remains a profound mystery.

Since the light is now gone, there's no time to read. I bundle up tightly in my cardboard, and at first sleep eludes me, as I can't help but continue to try to interpret what happened with the banshee. This 'event' will stay with me for a long time and with that thought I must have dosed off and fallen into a deep sleep. I wake up with a jolt and was surely dreaming, but I can't remember what about. It's another gloomy day and still cold, though not quite as brutal as before. I get up and go through some exercise routines to warm up a bit.

After this, my thoughts are directly steered towards reading. I look through several of the books piled up. What a treasure they are in the midst of such desolation. Just having them before me brings comfort.

While I love stories, I seem nowadays to be more and more attracted to poetry. Maybe this is an end of life kind of thing.

Who knows?

At any rate, I pick up one of the volumes I've already dipped into and now read more poetry written by Wordsworth.

Mutability

From low to high doth dissolution climb,
And sink from high to low, along a scale
Of awful notes, whose concord shall not fail;
A musical but melancholy chime,
Which they can hear who meddle not with crime,
Nor avarice, nor over-anxious care.
Truth fails not; but her outward forms that bear
The longest date do melt like frosty rime,
That in the morning whitened hill and plain
And is no more; drop like the tower sublime
Of yesterday, which royally did wear
His crown of weeds, but could not even sustain
Some casual shout that broke the silent air,
Or the unimaginable touch of Time.

The Prelude, Book 13.

Who doth not love to follow with his eye
The windings of a public way? the sight,
Familiar object that it is, hath wrought
On my imagination since the morn

Of childhood, when a disappearing line,
One daily present to my eyes, that crossed
The naked summit of a far off hill
Beyond the limits that my feet had trod,
Was like an invitation into space
Boundless, or guide into eternity.

And further on humanity:
Theirs is the language of the heavens, the power,
The thought, the image, and the silent joy
Words are but under-agents in their souls -

These tantalizing lines by Wordsworth are magnificent. Such exquisite concepts and words spark imagination and give rise to thought. They have a marvelous density and are seething with symbols and metaphors. Time, precious time, a mystery of past present, and future seems to have an 'unimaginable touch.' Beginnings and ends, and ends and beginnings – eternity beckons.

There are no perfect or complete words for any poem, story, or life, yet in spite of this, there is a measure of understanding and exposition that is possible, even vital for all three. Indeed, poetry rebels against the monotonous and a reductionistic use of words. It opens horizons far beyond the formal or scientific, ever reaching for the sublime and the expansion of meaning. While subversion can be risky, the richness of the poems, makes it worthwhile. William Wordsworth, the majestic poet, offers many insights and enigmas of what it means to be human in this world and may even have something to say that pertains to my present story. But that, I'd wager, is for the reader to decide.

As for me, I now sit with the book of poems on my lap and close my eyes.

What will unfold?

No idea.

I travel through time, engaging with words and scenes through the power of memory, imagination, and poetry, stopping along the way at one moment, before going on to the next and the next. Parts of my life flash before me, and an opaque light shines on a succession of narratives and events. It's like I'm an actor and observer at the same time. This flow of images, thoughts, and feelings however, goes far beyond my capacity to analyze and explain. Complex! The interpretation of my own life is an arduous task. The fissures of time slip by ever so slowly; so slowly, and they are difficult to grasp hold of. Brusquely, in the midst of these meanderings, the book slips off my lap with a thud, interrupting the recounting of the story. I open my eyes, pick up a book, and turn to read some lines from a poem by Philiss Wheatly, published around 1773.

On Imagination

Imagination! who can sing thy force?
Or who describe the swiftness of thy course?
Soaring through air to find the bright abode,
Th' empyreal palace of the thund'ring God,
We on thy pinions can surpass the wind,
And leave the rolling universe behind:
From star to star the mental optics rove,
Measure the skies, and range the realms above.
There in one view we grasp the mighty whole,
Or with new worlds amaze th' unbounded soul.

I'm mesmerized by these words, for how long I'll never know, and then read them again. Considering the date of this poem it is remarkably contemporary. I sense that it fits in with so many of my own musings.

Breathtaking!

The mysteries of imagination, space, and nature surface as major themes in Wheatley's superlative poem. Mixed metaphors create and refigure reality, offering a delicate balance between subversion and revelation. These wonderfully suggestive pictures open up imaginary dimensions of "possible worlds" that one can enter and maybe even dwell within.

Crushingly sublime!

Putting the book of poetry aside for a moment, I realize I'm chilly and it's cold. But strangely my distinct impression is that in fact it may be warming up again. Seems like these extreme climate changes and temperature variations are happening more rapidly than before. Cold and hot wildly fluctuate and I feel it in my bones. I wonder if this a sign of things to come. Probably, but everything is so unstable, it's hard to be sure of much of anything. While there is a large degree of ambiguity concerning my information and knowledge, what does appear evident is the horrific state of planet Earth.

Such a calamity! Such a tragedy!

What remains of it is awful, but I suppose it could get even worse.

My thoughts veer off in this depressing direction when suddenly, through an opening in the roof of the library, I hear a strange whooshing sound and look up. What I see absolutely astounds me! A transporter appears in the sky like a blur from the east. It's moving incredibly fast, but then slows and descends. Mind blowing. Freaking wild. It's sleek and smooth. Never seen anything like that. I'd wager, it will be landing at the Mars XXX site.

But for what?

Who knows?

Seems like some form of life has returned to planet Earth for something. Maybe searching for survivors, but I'm not sure. I need to go and find out what this is all about. I'm not thrilled about having to return to the industrial site, yet under the circumstances it's imperative to see if anyone or anything is there. I have tried to face the reality that I might be alone in the world, but doing so has taken its toll, leaving deep physical and emotional scars etched into my being. I'm scared, exhausted, and hoping for a change that might allow me to live differently, as it were, in an imaginatively "possible world" where 'all shall be well.' Perhaps, this is an opportunity to do that, but then again perhaps not. So, back I go. I start out from the library and remember the way to begin with, but then get a little disoriented and have to look around for one of my gray markers to make sure I'm still going in the right direction. You'd think I know the way by heart, but the devastated landscape all looks so similar, it's sometimes difficult to find my bearings. I don't want to get lost, especially now.

For the moment, I can only see the marker that I'm standing next to, and have to try going in several directions before I locate the next one and can proceed. It's starting to get hotter and I'd wager it will soon be torrid. My breathing is heavy and strength low. Tramping along I notice that my shoes are no longer absorbing the shock of walking through the hard rubble. They're worn out and need replacing, and my feet tell the story. Tired, and bruised. Maybe I can find some better shoes on the way to Mars XXX, but I probably don't want to mess around with this now.

I continue on and wend my way through some narrow passageways. When I come to what looks as if it's the last one, I'm surprised by a mysterious figure who suddenly appears in the sky. It's wearing a stunning rainbow colored robe and a black flowing cape. I don't see its head or face covered by a hood, nor its body, which seems to be hidden by the outrageous garments. Even though my top priority is to get back to Mars XXX as quickly as possible, I can't help but be transfixed by this exotic being or whatever it is, and I wonder why it's here. At this point, my trust and suspicion mode kicks in. Do I ignore this character and attempt to move on, or do I give in to my curiosity and wait to see what might happen? As always, decisions are hard to come by and I have to weigh things up. So far, this manifestation does not seem threatening or out to harm me, on the other hand, this may be a diversion tactic aimed to get me off course or worse, to take my life. My previous encounters have been a mixed bag, and through experience I know they're capable of good as well as bad.

I ponder: Why this presence now, when I'm rather in a hurry, to say the least?

Who knows?

On balance, I decide to privilege trust over suspicion and let my curiosity play its role. This may be a mistake, but what's taking place here is so exceptional that I'm interested in finding out, if possible, what's going on, so I'll roll the dice and take a chance.

I don't want to stay long, and hope to be on my way fairly soon, but just as I think this, I'm startled by the colorful character, who abruptly swoops down to the ground nearby and points me in the direction of what appears to be a vast burial ground. The tombstones are innumerable. A profound grief pierces through me, and I'm trembling inside as I gaze over this ghastly landscape of so many dead. Who were they? What happened to them? Then the black caped figure pulls back its hood, and a skull stares straight at me. There is no flesh, except what appears to be a massive brain like substance lodged smack in the middle of it.

Gruesomely stunning!

It seems to me to possess, from what I can tell, a powerfully built in GPS or something like that with a beam that searches for, illuminates, and then enhances distant objects and epitaphs. After the laser careens around and bounces off many different places, it finally settles on a tombstone, which it then magnifies: It has no name or birthdate, but something is written on it. For a spell, how long I'll never know, I'm in a state of deep perplexity. I eventually gather myself together some and am able to read the inscription:

> When you diligently search for a response to your situation, you sometimes find it.

The selfish human pursuit of power, domination, and control played a significant role in mass destruction. War, pollution, starvation, climate change, and pandemic, were all part of the multiple toxic catastrophes that took place in a short period of time and decimated all of life on planet Earth. The Earth became uninhabitable. Millions and millions died. Most humans didn't stand a chance and only a few escaped the devastation by heading into space, as the planet reached the point of collapse and no return.

My first reaction to the tombstone and its account of what happened is to ask whether I can trust it, or should I be suspicious of this data. Much of what it says seems to make sense; the written testimony does explain something of what I see (destruction) or don't see around me (other humans or human life forms). Thus, in spite of the bizarre circumstances of this rainbow clad character popping onto the scene, and zooming light on this huge cemetery, the revelation on the tombstone appears to be credible. It rings true, and therefore I wager it's trustworthy.

My longings or even demands for a black and white answer to this strange scenario will have to be replaced by that which I now have been given; a givenness that is not crystal clear. My thought is that this is the best I can do under the circumstances. Until I come across a more credible proposal, I'll hang onto this.

Wow!

According to the writing on the tombstone, by whom I have no idea, it conjectures that human greed, arrogance, and negligence are at the root of the numerous calamities that have destroyed Earth. I wonder if perhaps this view represents something of the future, the present, and the past. Alas, if so, again, the mystery of time.

Who knows?

My second reaction to the account of planet Earth's death written on the symbolical tombstone is intense and overwhelming sorrow! That humans played a significant role in their own demise and the destruction of their environment is heart breaking, and to envision the diversity of deadly consequences all taking place at the same time is chilling. I still find it mind blowing: Like a wild illusion.

After searching and searching for reliable "informers" as to why I'm alone in the world, I'm astonished that this "epitaph" was revealed to me by a rainbow robed and black caped one. So bizarre.

But then this comes to mind. During the course of millennia total destruction of humans and nature seemed impossible, however it appears that the 'impossible became possible.' Urgent appeals for change and new direction were ignored. The splendor, beauty, and complexity of billions of years now gone, as well as the much more recent phenomena of human beings. While several extinctions had previously taken place on Earth, none were ever the result, as it appears to be this time, of human folly. What a woeful tale and devastating tragedy for all of life on the planet.

My physical, emotional, and mental capacities to cope with this surprising series of events are frazzled. I put my face in my hands, bow my head, and just breakdown. Raw sensations that encompass anger, disappointment, regret, and frustration swirl around inside me, as well as deep musings about beginnings and endings.

This is heavy.

Wow!

Gradually I reset, but can't shake off these thoughts and emotions.

When I look up, the cemetery and the figure with the rainbow robe and black cape are gone, or at least out of my sphere of perception, or perhaps something else entirely. At any rate, it all disappeared, as if it never existed. This is weird and I don't have time to sort it out now, but I still hold onto trust over suspicion, and believe the data presented is a valid perspective for the moment.

When I look down, a pair of brand new rainbow colored heavy duty sneakers with black soles are laying in front of me. That's crazy; absolutely extraordinary. I put them on. A perfect fit.

What a marvel! Ah, small joys in the midst of troubled times!

I have no idea what to make of this, but I'll nonetheless take it. These shoes, of superior quality and aesthetic design, will be a blast to wear and also a huge help as I trek through the rubble, which seems never ending. They will also be a vivid reminder of the fascinating character, the wrenching icons of the dead, and the tombstone's explosive message.

Remarkable!

Still somewhat bedazzled by these dramatic events, I nevertheless remember that I better quickly get a move on. It's still sweltering and I have difficulty breathing. I refocus on locating the next of my gray markers, which will lead me to the industrial area, where I imagine the transporter has already landed. I look around and at first don't see anything. I figure I'll continue straight ahead for a couple of hundred meters, and if I can't locate one, I'll return and head off in a different direction.

As I start off again, after a few meters, I happen to glance to my left and notice a marker almost entirely covered by the debris. This is likely the result of the recent earthquakes moving stuff around. A shift of just a few meters makes a huge difference, as it was impossible to see from where I was standing at first. Indeed, a valuable find, since I could have wasted a lot of time searching all over for it. Following on from this spot, I locate one after the other and make good progress. Up ahead I now see a series of several cavern/tunnel type configurations, which freak me out. Caverns can be dangerous, and contain frightening surprises, as I already have experienced. I don't remember going through these last time I went to the industrial zone, and there is no visible marker to show me this is the right way, so maybe I need to be patient and look around more carefully before proceeding. If I can avoid the caverns, all the better. As I scan the landscape, there is no sign of any marker, so I guess I have no choice but to pass through the caverns. But when I move towards them, I'm overwhelmed by a deep sense of foreboding and my fear levels skyrocket. Instead of going on, I immediately turn away and retreat to my last marker. I feel better and more secure here, so I chill a bit. My breathing is still short and rapid, and it's difficult to inhale deeply without gasping. The air pollution is horrendous, and perhaps it's even getting worse, but I do need to carry on.

In the twinkle of an eye, a goblin with a shining face appears about fifty meters to my left, like out of a fairy tale. Dressed in a glittering green shirt, sparkling blue pants, and sporting a dazzling red trench coat, and a glitzy black fedora with a yellow feather in the band, the goblin scampers up some debris and starts to point toward the east, which is in the opposite direction of the caverns. This colorful apparition is puzzling and I'm not sure what to make of it. While I'd like to find another marker and avoid the caverns, I have no idea what the goblin is pointing to and whether I should trust or be suspicious of it. For now, I keep both in play.

I edge closer and go towards the east some, and even though I still don't see any marker, I keep on for a spell. Then the goblin moves another fifty meters ahead. It seems clear that I'm going to have to follow this brilliantly dressed shiny faced character meter by meter, but in doing so I risk going too far and not being able to get back to where I started. Thus, I find myself in a position where the necessity for trust becomes greater than suspicion. Not sure I like that, but perhaps I have no other choice, as maybe all my other markers leading to the site have been entirely covered in rubble anyway.

Who knows?

The goblin might.

This could all be a charade, or a deceptive ploy to mislead or even harm me. My suspicions haven't quite left me. But my strong desire to avoid the caverns, and the remarkable appearance of this scintillating goblin, combined with the pressure of rapidly getting to the industrial complex soon, push me towards trust.

After going back and forth, I decide to follow the indications of the goblin, who continues to direct me east. Rambling along for a spell, I eventually come to a partially collapsed building. The goblin is still ahead of me pointing the same way, but as I glance over to the west, just past the dilapidated structure, I see a gray marker. What a relief. I feel a tremendous weight off my shoulders. But now what? I'm unsure where to go, and face another difficult decision. Mysteriously, in the next instant and with much greater intensity, the goblin is frantically pointing to the east, and then abruptly disappears. Gone goblin. I must say, I'm not as surprised as I used to be by the appearings and vanishings of these extraordinary characters, yet it's still baffling. I wonder if the goblin was intentionally directing me both away from the caverns and the industrial region. And if so, to where and for what? It definitely was not pointing me to my marker. It's so difficult to decipher what is reliable and what is deceptive in these strange circumstances. I suppose, in this case, I'll never know. I can ponder all this later, but should now move on.

Unfortunately, the heat has become unbearable. It's scorching, and I'll have to find shade soon. I head off from my gray marker, then stop, look around, and see another one in the distance. Looks like I'm back on track. My progress is pretty slow, but steady. The new shoes are a huge help, and I'm so glad to have them. Trudging through all this rubble is complicated, especially in the intense heat, but the shoes are well padded and absorb the shocks better than it would have been otherwise, plus they're nice to look at. I'll take beauty wherever I can find it in this devastated landscape. I discover several more markers in succession, but still don't know how far I am from the industrial zone. Climbing over and going around piles of debris seems endless. I'm short of breath and dripping with sweat. I want to stop and rest, yet have to continue. I try to encourage myself, and I pick up the pace.

This seems to work and I sense an increase of energy. After going on and on, I finally come to several metal and concrete columns through which I make my way. Once I'm on the other side of these, I begin to make out off in the west, the vast ruins of the industrial area. It's an enormous relief to get this far. I see another marker about twenty meters away, and I should have no trouble locating the others as I close in on my destination. Consequently, my journey should now be easier, but I still have a long ways to go.

When I finally arrive at the massive Mars XXX complex, I immediately see the transporter, which has now indeed landed. It's spectacular. But it appears to be empty and no one is in the vicinity. I'm grateful it's still here and move closer to check it out. This transporter is remarkable and looks a lot more sophisticated than the one left behind at the site. Seems like monumental improvements were made in many sectors, including an advanced aerodynamic design and a marked increase in size. Absolutely incredible! But how did the transporter find its way to planet Earth with no pilot? Was it on auto-pilot, or directed by an ultra-sophisticated pre-programmed GPS, or something like that? Possibly, since navigation technologies had been relentlessly developed, it could have finally come to something like this: Self-driving transporters, which shuttled beings from Earth to a location somewhere in the cosmos.

All of a sudden the whole industrial site fills with a billowing blue and purple haze that swirls around for a spell, but then gradually dissipates. I vaguely distinguish someone or something, who/which seems to be moving around inside the massive transporter before me and then the door pops open in the blink of an eye. A figure stands at the entrance. I'm not sure what kind of being this is, but it looks like something between human and high tech machine: stainless steel, electrical circuitry, and flesh. If so, I'm not really surprised by this configuration. Perhaps, I'll finally find out what is going on in space. For a while, how long I'll never know, nothing happens. Then, this eX-human type character addresses me in a strange mechanistic voice. I receive a proposal, one I assume that was given to many before me and, as far as I can tell, one that many accepted: that of survival.

I imagine crowds of humans and perhaps others at this very site, waiting to leave a ravaged planet Earth, and join an alternate space community somewhere in the uni-multiverse.

This time though, I'm the only one here!

Then a different voice addresses me. This one is clearer, and almost pleasant. It seems to be coming from an embodied screen and is probably streaming through a loud speaker located on the transporter. I gear up to listen attentively.

At this point, things become more specific. The voice now tells me I have one chance to escape Earth and to survive into the distant future in outer space, living a forever life beyond imagination. But in order to do so, I must become an eX-human. Suddenly, a techno-sapien prototype is projected before my eyes. It speaks, acts, and is equipped to live in an alternate reality, and gives me a mini-picture of what a survival 'I' might look like, constructed in a different manner to join others of its kind. After this projection, the voice says that in the process of transformation many human traits will be modified and others completely lost. But with these changes, long term survival becomes a real possibility. I reflect on this. It makes sense that since flesh and blood decay and end in death, deep tech could potentially fill in and keep you alive, albeit in a quite different form and composition. Seems like a wonderful offer. However, the voice then adds that this conversion can only take place when alive – the dead cannot be reanimated. I understand. It's not as if I can wait to die and then be transformed. It has to be done now. Thus, a decision is obligatory. Take it or leave it. There's no other way. That's it. I must decide on the spot.

This is all about surviving!

Nothing else matters!

So, here I am again facing another trust and suspicion scenario. This internal dialogue seems such a big part of my life, but this time the stakes are immense. What am I to make of this offer from a voice seemingly out of nowhere? Of course, I should be suspicious, but again I'm almost forced to trust it. I ponder the 'who?' and 'why?' of the voice, and its ultimate source. Is this all a grand deception? But if it is, to what end? I don't really have any sufficient reason to doubt the voice, and from my observations and discoveries, especially what I found in the tubes and cabinet, the space option sure looks like it had become a "possible world" for those wanting to flee the Earth and survive.

At this point, trust starts to outweigh suspicion. The voice has confirmed some of what I already suspected had been going on here, and thus has a ring of truth, as far as I can tell. I decide to trust that some form of survival is credible. But does that mean I should embrace it?

For me the choice is not about surviving at any cost, but about what it means to stay human up until death. As it was in the beginning, so it will be at the end. Even though humans have many faults and physical weaknesses, and we all without exception breakdown and die, something that looks like planned obsolescence. Nevertheless, I don't think I want to be revised, recharged, and remodeled into a mere force for survival. After all, there is also something special about being human, including relationality, imagination, memory, creativity, and emotions such as, joy, fear, anger, sadness, love, and hope, all of which would be drastically modified or lost in transformation. I need time to carefully think through the prospect of losing so much of what identifies me.

But when it comes down to it, who cares?

Why would it matter?

Surely, some form of existence is better than none?

What should I do?

What would anybody do?

These questions and others plague me to the core. I'm torn about this. I've never ever faced such an excruciating decision. I already have so much difficulty making up my mind about the simplest of things. Now this! Deep and careful reflection is vital. I keep going through the positives and negatives, and wrangle with different angles. I feel I'm under a massive amount of pressure. I continue to go back and forth, back and forth. I bat it around, and around, and around.

And then my decision is made. I refuse the offer. This is automatically understood and accepted by whoever/whatever is in the transporter. There are no demands, no threats, no arguments, and absolutely no further interaction with it/them at all. I watch the door of the transporter close, and in the blink of an eye, it vanishes at lightning speed, probably never to return.

After this happens, I fall to my knees shaking and weeping uncontrollably. The sheer physical, mental, and emotional weight of the decision, and all it entailed, is humanly staggering. It takes some time, how long I'll never know, to regain my composure and prepare for what's next.

As for me, I will continue to live here on Earth, and read stories and poetry, and who knows what else I might find on my explorations. I will continue to struggle with and embrace human life from one day to the next, for as long as I can, until I die.

Now to find my way back to the library before it gets darker.